MADAME MUSTACHE

ORPHAN
RUNAWAYS

KRISTIANA GREGORY

SCHOLASTIC PRESS

NEW YORK

Copyright © 1998 by Kristiana Gregory
Frontispiece courtesy Amon Carter Museum, Fort Worth, Texas

Library of Congress Cataloging-in-Publication Data

Gregory, Kristiana.
Orphan runaways / Kristiana Gregory.
p. cm.
Summary: Harrowing adventures accompany twelve-year-old Danny
and his younger brother Judd when they run away from a San Francisco
orphanage and search for their uncle in a gold rush boomtown.

ISBN 0-590-60366-3

[1. Brothers—Fiction. 2. Orphans—Fiction. 3.
Gold mines and mining — Fiction.] I. Title.
PZ7.G8619Or 1998
[Fic] — dc21 97-4345
CIP AC

1 2 3 4 5 6 7 8 9 10   03 02 01 0/0 9/9 8

Printed in the U.S.A.
First edition, March 1998
Design by David Caplan

GRE

CONTENTS

59299

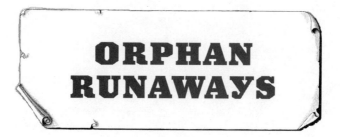

ORPHAN
RUNAWAYS

SHORE ACRES ORPHANAGE

DANNY O'REILLY lay quietly in bed, watching the rats. There were five on his side of the dormitory, gray and as big as cats, crawling along the damp windowsills.

Every evening they came through a hole in the wall, first a few, then as it grew dark, more. Their claws clicking along the bare floor kept Danny awake with nervousness. What could the creatures possibly be searching for? For he knew there was no food, not a crumb. Mr. Lowry wouldn't permit it.

"A beating for a biscuit," he warned the orphans at supper, should they try to hide bread in their pockets.

The long, narrow room held forty beds. Danny was thankful his was under a window, for when the others were asleep he pulled himself up to look out. Three stories below were the cobbled streets of San Francisco, lit dimly by gas lamps. A carriage passed, then rounded a corner to the Opera House, the horses elegant and high-stepping.

Danny heard sobs from the bunk next to his and knew it was his little brother. Judd was six years old, the youngest in this wing of Shore Acres. He knelt by Judd's bed and took the boy in his arms.

"Don't cry," he whispered. "Mr. Lowry will hear and he'll whip you again. Please, Judd . . ."

A door at the end of the room swung open and as light spread across the floor, the rats scattered under beds. Someone held up a candle.

Before the light reached Danny, he quickly knelt by his own bunk.

"You there!" It was the angry voice of Mr. Lowry. "What are you doing, O'Reilly?"

Danny shivered with fear and with cold for the room was unheated. "Sir, I'm praying."

The headmaster held up the candle to see the two brothers better. Danny saw with relief that Judd's eyes were closed in pretend sleep.

"What on earth would a lad such as yourself need to pray about?"

"A family, sir." Danny swallowed. He wasn't telling a lie, because even though he hadn't at that exact moment been praying, he did every day, every hour almost.

2

"Well, then. Since you enjoy being on your knees so much you can spend the morning scrubbing the steps outside. No breakfast. Maybe you'll stop whimpering and thank me for giving you a home. Get in bed."

Danny cringed, waiting for the hand to strike, but suddenly the room was dark and he heard the headmaster's boots stomping downstairs. He was too afraid to whisper. Lying on his side he reached out from under his blanket to touch his brother's bed six inches away.

Judd's small hand clutched his, and only when they became too cold did they tuck their arms back under their own blankets.

Danny felt in his shirt pocket for his mother's wedding ring. He touched it for comfort and remembered how it shone on her slender hand as she played the piano. Now as he drifted toward sleep, the clicking of rats' claws became the clicking of her metronome. He saw her lovely face and he saw his father smiling at her. Somewhere in Danny's dream he also saw the cradle where his sister slept.

How could any of them have known an epidemic would soon sweep the city; that 1878 would become known as the Year of the Orphan?

A NEW FAMILY

"MY, MY," said the lady as she untied her bonnet. She stood by her husband in the dining hall, looking over the rows of children waiting permission to eat their porridge. The boys were scrubbed clean with parted hair, and the girls wore braids. Their faces were thin.

The lady turned to Mr. Lowry and whispered, "But there're so many to choose from."

"Yes, indeed. We take only the best, no Chinese or coloreds, of course."

After the meal, Danny was carrying coal to the headmaster's office when he passed Mr. Lowry on the stairs with the couple.

"Adoption is easy," Mr. Lowry was explaining. "Just say which one and I'll have papers drawn up immediately. For that matter, you can take home ten of the little dumplings if you can stand them. Come in, please."

He took off his hat and hung it with his coat, then motioned for the couple to sit.

As Danny poured coal into the grate, Mr. Lowry rolled open the top of his desk and dipped his pen into a pot of ink. With a flourish he wrote in a ledger, then blew on the page until it dried. He smiled at the lady and said, "Shall we get down to business?"

"What is the name of that littlest boy," she asked softly, "the one whose cap kept slipping over his eyes?"

"Madam, a good choice. O'Reilly is his name, Judd O'Reilly. His father was Irish, his mother's grandpa fought with George Washington in the Revolution. A rather good bloodline, I'd say."

Danny felt his heart race. So surprised was he to hear Judd's name, he dropped the bucket.

"Missus," Danny said, "please, there are three of us. Judd is my brother. Our sister is nine months old."

Mr. Lowry raised himself out of his chair and pointed to the rug now black with soot. "After you clean this, you'll report to the courtyard where you shall be taught some manners. Madam, ignore this child. As you can see, many of the urchins who come to us haven't been taught a blessed thing. They're spoiled, stupid, and selfish." Saying this he turned a cold eye on Danny.

Danny tightened his fist and for an instant wanted to hit the headmaster, but he held his temper. He didn't want to ruin their chance to be adopted. As he bent down to scoop up the coal, his face burned with anger. Mother and Father did too teach him manners.

"I apologize, sir." Then he looked up at the lady who was brushing dust off her dress. How could he make her understand that he had promised Judd they would stay together no matter what?

The next morning Danny again was denied breakfast so he could polish the long, twisted banister of the front stairs. He was hungry and his head ached from lack of sleep. When he heard familiar voices, he looked over the rail, down to the marbled entrance.

It was the couple from the day before. Danny couldn't see their faces, just the wide flowered brim of the lady's hat and the crown of her husband's derby. They were chatting happily when Mr. Lowry walked up to them, holding the hand of a child.

Instantly Danny recognized Judd's cap and blond hair curling at the neck. He set down his rag and jar of oil, careful not to spill any this time. With his hand on the rail he leaned over to listen while quietly stepping down the stairs.

"He's a good boy, madam," said the headmaster. "You and your husband will have no troubles, I assure you."

She took Judd's hand and smiled. "Would you like a puppy, darling?"

Her husband leaned down also to smile. "Son, how would you like to go for a sail on a real three-masted schooner. How about it?"

"He's afraid of the ocean, sir," came Danny's voice. He stood on the bottom stair. "I'm Judd's brother. Please take me, too, and our sister."

Their smiles dropped at the sight of Danny. His legs were too long for his pants so there was a gap between his cuffs and the tops of his shoes. He was thin and lacked the rosy cheeks of his little brother.

"Hey, Dan!" cried Judd. He tried to run to him, but Mr. Lowry stepped between them. He spoke to the couple.

"This older boy is twelve, old enough to work for his living, so he need not burden a family, madam. We have plenty for him to do here. This little one, on the other hand, needs a mother immediately. As for their sister, she's with the nuns at Saint Mary's."

Danny stepped forward, but Mr. Lowry laid a heavy hand on his shoulder until the couple had hurried out the door with Judd. Waiting at the curb was a carriage with a driver holding the reins tight.

When the lady lifted her hem to step up, Judd turned around to look for his brother. "Danny!" he wailed, suddenly realizing they were to be separated. At this, Danny twisted away from Mr. Lowry, bolted down the steps to the sidewalk, and grabbed Judd's arm.

"Now you listen here," the husband said, reaching for the driver's whip. He swung it overhead with a crack, but missed the boys as they dashed behind the coach and into the crowded street.

Shouts and curses came from the headmaster as he ran after them. When a vegetable cart pulled out from an alley, blocking his path, he threw down his hat and cursed again.

THE RUNAWAYS

FOG SETTLED OVER THE CITY, a gray mist that made the boys' shirts damp. They had wandered two miles from the orphanage and now found themselves at the harbor where the strong smell of salt water reminded Danny of home.

Their last family outing had been a few weeks before, a summer picnic at the beach. Father had explored the tide pools with them, while Mother watched from a blanket, baby Susanna playing in the sand with a rope of seaweed. At this memory, Danny's eyes filled and he turned away so Judd wouldn't see him cry.

He must be brave. He must think carefully what to do.

They came to a row of houses facing the wharf. The tall windows glowed with candlelight and there was a delicious aroma of cooking. Because Danny hadn't eaten since last night's supper he felt desperate with hunger.

Holding Judd's hand he walked up to a porch where there was a baby carriage among a clutter of toys. The door was opened by a dark-haired woman wiping her hands on her apron. Her face was kind, but she spoke to them in a language they didn't understand. Finally she called over her shoulder, "Antonio!" and motioned the boys inside.

The house was warm and busy with children, seven Danny counted, and an infant sleeping in a box by the stove. The children erupted in laughter when their father Antonio entered the room, for sitting on his head was a monkey. It wore a tiny red vest and was clapping its hands.

Danny recognized the organ-grinder, a cheerful man who had visited the orphanage the week before. If he knew the boys were runaways, he didn't let on, but spoke rapidly to his family. An older girl set two more plates on the table.

"Thank you so much," Danny said many times that evening, especially when the mother led them out back to a small stable where she made them beds of clean straw.

Some hours later Danny bolted awake. It was dark, but there were voices. He peeked through a crack in the wall and saw that a lantern was being carried through the house toward the back porch. When the kitchen door opened, Danny gasped, for there was the headmaster and two constables.

Antonio was in his nightshirt, pointing toward the harbor saying, "The boys not here . . . boys gone . . ."

The lantern swung shadows across the yard as the men walked toward the stable. Danny covered Judd's mouth with his hand and pulled him up, trying to see in the slivered light where to hide. They crawled under a shelf, through the straw to a corner where there was a large knothole in the wood.

"Don't worry, Mr. Lowry, we'll find them if it takes all night." The voice was near.

Danny took a deep breath. He kicked at the hole — once . . . twice . . . three times — until the board split apart and he could push Judd out. He squeezed behind him, just as the barn filled with light.

Shouts followed the brothers as they ran through the darkness.

When at last they stopped to rest, hiding under a stairway, Danny made a decision.

He would never again let the headmaster beat him nor try to take Judd away. They must flee San Francisco. He felt anguished to leave baby Susanna behind, but knew she'd be safe with the nuns. If he could just reach his relatives somehow, one of them could help the boys return for her.

Their grandparents lived in Oregon City. Aunt Hattie and Uncle Wade ran a dairy near Portland and another uncle was captain of a lumber ship. Three other uncles worked in California at various mining camps, but how to reach any of these places, Danny didn't know.

Because news traveled slowly, the family probably hadn't heard about the influenza epidemic, or that Mother and Father were dead.

Danny suddenly felt sick inside. No one who cared about them knew they'd been orphaned.

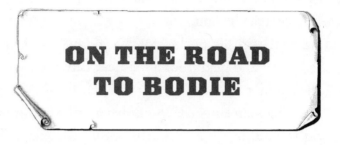

ON THE ROAD TO BODIE

IT WAS STILL DARK when the milk wagons began making their rounds. Danny woke to the *clop-clop* of horses and the *clang* of milk cans being set on porches. He crawled out from the stairs and looked downhill toward the harbor. This gave him an idea, but they must hurry.

He woke Judd. Near the wharf was a livery stable with a sign: SAN FRANCISCO FERRY AND FREIGHT. An office next door had a window, yellow with candlelight. They peered inside. A man stood warming himself in front of a stove.

Danny tapped on the glass. The man came over and slid open the small window.

"Where to?" he asked.

"Oregon City," said Danny.

The man licked his thumb to flip through a book. "Stagecoach is twenty-three dollars and seventy-five cents one way." He looked at them over the tops of his glasses. "Each," he said.

Danny felt in his pocket for his mother's ring. He pulled it out and held it for a moment before setting it on the counter.

"Ha," the man laughed. "Son, this may be worth the world to you, but it ain't worth one ticket outa Californee, that's the truth."

There was a catch in Danny's throat. He put his arm around Judd who stood sleepily at his side. Behind them were sounds of a city beginning to waken and a sky growing lighter by the moment. He worried the headmaster might find them.

Suddenly he remembered the address of Uncle Hank. "Will it get us to Bodie?" he asked.

The man began to laugh, but stopped himself. He leaned over to get a better look at the boys. Their hair was damp from the mist and they looked cold. As he rolled the ring between his fingers he remembered the epidemic.

"Got family in Bodie, do you?"

"Yessir."

The man stamped two tickets with the date — September 4, 1878 — and opened a side door where a large scale hung from the rafters. "Here's what we're gonna do, fellas . . . up you go. Next freight wagon

14

leaves in ten minutes. You," he said to Judd, lifting him back to the ground, "weigh exactly fifty-one pounds. At two cents a pound that'd be about one dollar. Let's call it three dollars for the both of you, with some change back."

He pulled a small leather pouch from his vest and took out two silver coins, which he placed in Danny's palm.

"You'll need a little something for food. Bodie's due east, almost to the Nevada border, so it could take three-four days, depending on weather and bandits. But I guess you already know Bodie is the wildest, meanest, godforsaken mining camp in the West and cold as the devil — it's clear up in the mountains, about eighty-six hundred feet above sea level. And there ain't even a church."

The first day out of San Francisco it rained fourteen hours straight. Danny and Judd lay under a tarp at the rear of the wagon, where mud spattered up from the bumping wheels. The driver seemed unconcerned that his cargo of U.S. mail and whiskey barrels also included two young boys.

When they stopped near Lake Tahoe to change mules, Danny pushed back the muddy tarp. He saw rolling hills with pine trees and miles of open space. The air was cool.

Once again his hunger was fierce. He led Judd to a cottage and knocked. He held out his hand to show the woman his coin, but she snatched it and slammed the door.

The boys were too astonished to speak. Danny tried to think. He knocked again.

"Ma'am, may we buy some bread, please?" he called. While they stood under the dripping eaves, for it had begun to rain again, they heard a shout from the corral.

Their driver was already on his seat, reins in hand, calling to his mules. Slowly the animals pulled the wagon out onto the puddled road.

The boys ran. Danny boosted his brother into the back, then with a jump grabbed a rail to pull himself up.

As they held the tarp over their heads and watched the cottage grow smaller, a girl on horseback appeared. In a full gallop her cape flew out behind her. She came alongside the wagon and tossed a bundle to Danny, which he caught by its string. It was a blanket wrapped around three loaves of bread, but before he could thank her, she turned her horse and was gone.

*   *   *

When the sun finally came out, the boys sat on top of a mail sack to look around. In the distance were snowy peaks. Danny knew they were climbing in altitude because there were fewer trees and he felt slightly out of breath. Now he also learned why the driver had been making stops in the middle of nowhere.

Danny watched him walk around the side of the wagon and kiss one of the whiskey barrels. Carefully, he hammered an iron hoop upward, drove a nail into the wood, then wiggled the nail free.

Out gushed a stream of golden liquid. The man opened his mouth and drank until his beard and shirt were soaked, then he plugged the hole with a wad of chewing tobacco. Hammering the hoop down, he glared at the boys.

"Shaddup," he said. "A fella's gotta wet his whistle once in a while."

Through the next day and night, Danny and Judd tried to keep warm under their blanket, but it itched with fleas and the air was growing colder as the road twisted higher into the mountains. The cold made them feel even hungrier.

Finally they rounded a hill and drove into a noisy mining camp. In front of one of the saloons was a sign that said: AURORA, NEVADA, ELEVATION 7500 FT. Here the driver got down and stumbled through the swinging doors.

Danny was nervous about leaving the wagon this time so he called to a man watering his horse, "Mister, how much farther to Bodie?"

The man spit in the dirt. "Well, sonny, it's twelve miles west, just over the border to Californee. If you ain't held up by thieves and if that driver don't run you off a cliff, you might get there by midnight, but don't count on it."

CAPTAIN BILLY

MOONLIGHT LIT THE ROAD to Bodie, a narrow climb through a canyon and around hills that were carved with tunnels and mine shafts. The brothers huddled together in the back of the wagon where they were protected from the wind, the blanket pulled up to their chins. They were both hungry and exhausted.

As Danny lay watching the stars, his breath made steam in the cold air. How beautiful the night is, he thought. How good it will be to have a home again.

He'd met Uncle Hank a few years before, but couldn't recall what he looked like. What if he was mean? Did he have a wife and children now? All he remembered was that he was one of their mother's three brothers, from a family that came west on the Oregon Trail.

As the wagon bumped along under the starry sky, Danny began to feel nervous. He'd forgotten to consider one thing:

What if Uncle Hank didn't want them?

A noise in the distance distracted him, a pounding, like the slow beat of a drum. When he pulled himself up to look over the barrels, a cold wind hit his face. The pounding came from Bodie's stamp mill two miles away, where ore was crushed day and night.

The road dipped around a bluff and approached a brightly lit town. There were men on ladders hammering roofs, wagons hauling up and down Main Street; piano music mingled with shouts. It was two o'clock in the morning.

In front of Clara's Boardinghouse, the driver yelled to his mules to stop. He tried to climb down from his seat but was so drunk he toppled forward and fell into a pile of warm manure. He lay motionless as three men stepped over him to lift out the mail sacks, which they carried to the Wells Fargo office.

A crowd swarmed over the wagon and began unloading the barrels, and rolling them along the wooden sidewalks into various taverns. No one seemed to notice Danny and Judd standing by the mules.

No one except a boy leaning in the doorway of the Can-Can Saloon. He was ten years old and quietly smoking a cigar. He squinted through his smoke to watch the newcomers. Soon a man wearing a Confederate hat dragged the drunk driver out of the street, hauled him into the back of the wagon, then led the mules away.

Judd pressed close to Danny's side. When a rough hand pushed them, Danny swung around with his fist, ready to defend them, but saw it was just the boy with the cigar who was younger and smaller than he.

"Come with me if you want some grub," the boy said.

Danny didn't know what else to do, so he took Judd's hand and followed the boy down the noisy street. They stepped around a man sprawled in the mud, then up to the sidewalk. Suddenly two saloon doors swung open and out flew another man, his arms and legs flailing. Shouts followed, then several gunshots. A woman screamed.

The boys hurried by. Danny tried to see inside, but the room was filled with gun smoke. They passed several saloons loud with voices and music; there were cafes and a grocery store before they came to the Occidental Hotel. Two Paiutes with blankets over their shoulders sat on a bench out front; Danny tried not to stare at them, but he'd never seen Indians.

The door opened into a brightly lit lobby. Two cats slept in the middle of a billiard table. Against the wall was a mirror with angels carved into its frame. It hung over a bar where there were rows of bottles and glasses. A black man wiping the counter looked up and smiled. He said, "Well, Smokey Joe, who'd you bring me today?"

Joe took his cigar out of his mouth. "Fellas," he said to Danny and Judd, "this here is Captain Billy O'Hara — used to drive a Mississippi riverboat. His pap was a slave so don't mind his color."

At the sight of the two forlorn brothers, Captain Billy said, "Sit down, boys. First you eat, then we talk." He set a round loaf of bread on the counter and cut it into chunks, spread butter on top, added slices of beef, then poured two mugs of hot, strong coffee.

When Danny told their story, Captain Billy shook his head. "I sure is sorry for your troubles, but you was smart not to bring your baby sister here," he said. "This camp's full of miners that come and go, hundreds and hundreds, miners that get kilt on the job, miners that get shot, you name it. There is five thousand people in Bodie, but I ain't yet heard of Hank Valentine."

Judd turned to Danny and burst out, "Let's go back, Dan. That lady was going to give me a puppy."

Danny ate in silence. This was a stupid idea, he thought. They should've headed for Oregon, even if it would have taken weeks to earn their way from farm to farm.

A tall wooden clock in the corner chimed three. In a few hours the sun would rise. Captain Billy left the room and returned with two blankets, which he spread under the billiard table. "Here you go, boys. It'll be warmer here. Sleep on your worries. Tomorrow's a new day and we can start looking for your uncle."

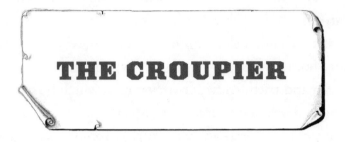

THE CROUPIER

DANNY WOKE TO SUNLIGHT streaming in a window. He'd slept badly on the hardwood floor, and he was chilled because of drafts from the front door opening and closing all night long. He needed to use the outhouse, but didn't want to wake Judd who was curled against him like a puppy.

From their bed under the table he could see only the boots and pant legs of customers coming and going. He tried to imagine Uncle Hank: Would he wear Levi's with boots or fine linen trousers with fine leather shoes? Danny didn't know if his uncle was a miner, a banker, or a bum.

Just then he realized that two men at the bar were fighting. Dust raised up as the feet shuffled and kicked, and stools fell over. Suddenly there was a gunshot. A pair of knees bent lower and lower until they dropped.

With a thud, a man fell to the floor inches away from Danny, blood seeping from a wound in his neck. The lifeless eyes stared at Danny. Horrified, he pulled Judd closer and tried to scoot away from the body.

There were shouts as the murderer ran out. Moments later someone took the dead man's arm and dragged him to the sidewalk, leaving a trail of bright red blood.

Danny was frightened and wondered if he should do something. He looked around the room. Asleep near the stove was the small form of Smokey Joe.

"'Allo, 'allo?" came a high voice. Danny saw a lady's dress come through the front door. The hem was ruffled with lace, and there was a flash of her ankles as she walked briskly past, stepping over the blood as if to do so was an everyday event. Her shoes were blue satin with tiny heels.

"Good morning, Madame," called Captain Billy, carrying a tray of tea from the kitchen.

At the sound of the woman's voice, Judd stirred. "Mama?" he whispered, trying to focus on his brother's face.

"Judd, we're in Bodie, remember? Come." They crawled out from under the table to warm themselves by the stove.

The woman had carried in a basket of fresh crois-sants, which she put on the bar. Out came a wedge of cheese and some apple tarts. She hummed to herself.

Danny wanted to buy breakfast, but he felt it would be impolite to ask since someone had just been killed, murdered right before his eyes — it bothered him that everyone seemed so calm. A boy his age came with a bucket of water and kneeled to scrub the bloody floor. He kept his eyes on his work, now and then glancing up at the brothers with curiosity.

"'Allo, Buster," the woman said to him. "Such a brave boy you are to do such a dir-tee job. I give you a candy when you are done."

She smiled at him sympathetically, then laid food on the counter while chatting to Captain Billy. Her French accent was pleasant.

Captain Billy walked over to kiss her cheek. "You, Madame, are more lovely every day," he told her. "Come meet our new friends."

When she turned around to face them, Judd hid be-hind his brother's back. Danny's mouth dropped open.

The woman had soft brown hair swept high on her head, green eyes, and a blush on her cheeks. Her dress was satin with a lace neckline, and its bustle flattered her small figure. What startled the boys was the mus-tache on her upper lip, a real mustache that curled at the ends. She didn't seem bothered by their reaction, but instead bent to touch Danny's cheek, then Judd's.

"Oh, you sweet, sweet boys. But where are your pair-ents?"

While they told their story, she settled into one of the armchairs and watched them tenderly. She patted her lap for Judd to come sit, which he did immediately. She held him in her arms as if he were her own child.

"If your un-cull is here, we will find him, don't you worry, darlings. Then we'll help get your sis-tair back."

Danny felt uneasy. He was still recovering from the shock of seeing a murder and now his own brother was letting himself be mothered by a complete stranger, a woman he'd not seen the likes of before.

Captain Billy noticed his discomfort. "Madame is our favorite croupier," he said to Danny, trying to reassure him. "That means she runs the game tables down at the Magnolia Saloon. She is honest and hardworking. She do not cuss in English, and she is the best lady gambler in the West, yessir."

Danny couldn't take his eyes off her mustache. Was he the only one who noticed and was it real? One thing he did know: She might be pretty and she might be smart, she might be the best croupier around, but he was not going to sit on her lap.

THE SEARCH BEGINS

BUSTER AND SMOKEY JOE also were orphans. Their fathers had been killed a few weeks earlier when the ore cart they were riding broke its cable and plunged to the bottom of Mono shaft. The tragedy was made worse because the boys were already without mothers. This was why Captain Billy took care of them, as he did other stray children who wandered in and out of the Occidental Hotel.

He painted a shingle that read:

ATTENTION HANK VALENTINE

INQUIRE WITHIN

IMPORTANT

As he hammered it to the front door he said, "Danny, you're big enough to know that any tramp can pretend to be your uncle, then treat you bad, or look for inheritance money. I will make plum sure no one takes you who ain't s'posed to. There." He gave the nail one last smack and stood back to admire his work.

Captain Billy's shirt was a light blue cotton, open at the neck with the sleeves rolled above his elbows, his skin black as ebony. His face was rugged, but when he smiled there was a softness that made Danny feel safe.

"Now run 'long, boys," he said. "If you back by sundown, there be supper waiting for you."

Bodie looked like a camp that wanted to be a town. Its side streets mushroomed with tents. Several stores and cafes had only canvas for roofs, and many saloons showed blue sky straight up. Everywhere men were nailing up walls, putting hinges on doors, and setting glass into window frames, trying to finish their buildings before winter set in.

No one paid attention to the O'Reilly brothers as they wandered up Main Street, which was as noisy as a carnival. Miners in muddy boots clomped along the planked sidewalks where the banging of hammers was heard at nearly every address. Shingles with new store names were being hung from awnings.

Hurrying among the crowd were Chinese men. Some pushed laundry carts, others carried poles on their shoulders with baskets on each end. They shouted to one another in their language, their long pigtails swaying across their backs. There was the jingle of harnesses and the rattle of wagons bumping over mud holes. Every so often the ground trembled from dynamite exploding in tunnels beneath their feet.

Even above this noise was the distant beat of the stamp mill.

For an hour Danny tried to study every face, hoping to see a man who resembled his mother — if such a thing were possible — but he soon grew weary. Judd stayed close, occasionally clinging to his brother's sleeve.

At Boone's General Store Danny stopped to look in the window. A woman holding a baby girl was having a bolt of cloth measured for her. Danny watched longingly, pretending for a moment it was his mother and Susanna. He suddenly felt aware of his stained shirt and torn trousers. He wished he had a cap like Judd's to hide his hair because it was oily and uncombed.

Main Street was one mile long, mostly saloons and billiard halls. When they had walked to the end where the road to Aurora began, Danny looked back. Far to the west was a sharp ridge of mountains, the Sierra Nevada, already frosted with snow.

This boomtown called Bodie was miles from nowhere, in a high desert surrounded by brown hills, not a tree in sight. Wind hissed through the sagebrush and blew sand over their shoes. It was the loneliest place Danny'd ever seen.

What if we can't find Uncle Hank? he thought. What then?

The air was growing cold so they headed back into town. They stopped in front of Clara's Boardinghouse. A sign by the front door read, LADIES AND GENTLEMEN: REST ASSURED WE EMPLOY NO COOLIES.

Danny knew "coolie" was slang for Chinese, but he was too distracted with hunger to wonder what the sign meant. There was a delicious smell of roast beef and fresh baked bread. A window framed with lace curtains reflected their thin figures. Mirrored behind them were wagons and men on horseback.

"Danny, let's go in here, can we?" Judd said.

They stepped inside and when the door closed it swallowed the noise of the street. There now was soft piano music and polite voices. All the tables were occupied except for one by the window where they could look out at the passing crowd.

One night after going to the symphony, their mother and father had taken the boys to one of San Francisco's finest restaurants, at the Palace Hotel. Waiters carrying domed platters had served their food while a violinist serenaded them. It had been an elegant evening.

Danny remembered what to do.

He pulled out a chair for his brother, unfolded the linen napkin, tucked it under Judd's chin, then went to the other chair and did the same for himself. He put his hands in his lap and smiled across the table.

"So, Judd, here we are, just like old times. Order anything you want," he said, imitating their father.

Danny had just one coin left. He knew they needed warm clothes and they should pay Captain Billy for letting them stay with him. Also, tomorrow they would need to buy food again. But for the moment he didn't care. They were hungry and cold and weary, and for just this once he wanted to do something familiar, something to help them remember their parents.

"Well?" came a voice. Danny looked up to see a girl his age with red hair braided over her shoulders and an apron that covered her dress.

"Yes, miss," he replied, "we'll have the Special. Two, please."

She narrowed her eyes and put a hand on her hip. "Show me your money first," she said.

As Danny reached into his pocket, a voice came from the kitchen, "Stella Marie, be nice."

Stella rolled her eyes. "Yes, Aunt Clara," she said, then leaning over the table she whispered, "If you little worms don't pay, I'll twist your necks off."

A GRUESOME GAME

THAT NIGHT DANNY AND JUDD again slept under the pool table. It was drafty, but safe. With so many people coming and going at least they wouldn't be stepped on. The boys fell asleep to the crack of billiard balls rolling overhead. They were too tired to be bothered by the men who walked back and forth around the table with cue sticks.

At sunrise, an explosion startled the boys awake. They hurried to look out the front window. The street was lined with flags, some were the Stars and Stripes, some were the flag of Mexico. Two men on horseback were racing each other down opposite sidewalks, yelling and shooting pistols up into the wooden awnings.

Captain Billy brought a tray with gingerbread and mugs of cocoa. "It's Hidalgo Day, boys, eat some breakfast. Don't ask me why, but since I been in Bodie, every September 19 and every May 5 the Messicans have parties. Don't ask me why. There is big doin's down yonder, baseball games, dogfights, and such. Smokey Joe and Buster can take you there after chores."

At the western edge of town there were two roads, one leading to Bridgeport, the other around Mono Lake to Mammoth City. Several wagons had brought visitors to the flats where an event of great interest was about to take place.

Danny and Judd followed a gang of boys to where a man with a shovel was digging a hole out in the center of a field. A cowboy wearing spurs and chaps carried over a live rooster, set it in the hole, then buried it up to its neck.

"What are they doing to the chicken?" Judd asked, looking at Danny with worry. "They won't hurt it, will they, Dan?"

They had grown up with parents of refined tastes; after all, Father had been a tenor with the San Francisco Opera. The most brutal thing they'd ever seen was when a fisherman caught a great white shark and hung it by its tail on the wharf. Danny didn't know what would happen to the rooster, but he felt it wouldn't be good.

Smokey Joe didn't seem worried. He puffed on his cigar, his thumbs hooked in his suspenders. Buster stood at his side, a shy boy who looked as if he didn't know what to do with himself. He quietly watched as horses and riders gathered at each end of the field.

A man with a sombrero tied under his chin so the wind wouldn't blow it off yelled through a tin horn. A gunshot started the race, *Correr el gallo*. Danny soon realized the winner would be the first horseman to reach down and pull the rooster up by its neck. He took Judd's hand and walked behind the row of spectators so he wouldn't see.

Several fancy women stood high up on wagon seats for a better view. They clapped and cheered in such a coarse way Danny guessed they were saloon dancers. Further away were Chinese men wearing smocks over black cotton pants. The fronts of their heads were shaved. With them was a Chinese girl, who looked about eighteen years old and pretty. Her black hair hung to her waist. Standing close to her was a miner. The two glanced at each other with such tenderness Danny wondered if they were sweethearts.

When he smelled the stink of a cigar he knew Smokey Joe had found him. Joe pointed to the girl and spoke loud enough for her to hear.

"Don't trust Chinese," he told the brothers. "One trip

into Chinatown, you'll know what I mean. You'll smell what I mean. Any man that goes after a China girl ain't a man, he's a first-class chump, that's what my pa always said, a chump."

At this the miner turned around. "You best be moving along, young fellow. Go on now," he said, taking the girl's hand affectionately.

She also turned, but said nothing. When her eyes fell on Judd, her face softened. The boy's cheeks were chapped from the dry air and he was shivering with cold. She reached forward to touch him, but he was pulled away by Smokey Joe, who cussed at the man and girl.

Tapping ashes into the dirt, he said to his new friends, "Everyone knows it's against the law for whites to marry Chinese."

A NEW PLAN

Music from the Can-Can Saloon was so loud it spilled out into the street. Danny noticed a menu in the window. Above the prices, in big letters, it said: NO CHINA COOKS EMPLOYED. This was a sign he'd seen in many of the cafes.

Inside by the warm stove a fiddler played "John Brown's Body" for two miners dancing on a table. Plates and spoons bounced to the floor as their friends clapped along. On the balcony overhead several men involved in a fistfight were shouting and cursing. Danny and Judd watched with fascination as one of them tumbled downstairs and another fired his six-shooter into the ceiling. Meanwhile the bartender calmly wiped whiskey glasses with his towel.

Smokey Joe called to the brothers from the kitchen where he was making sandwiches. "Help yourselves, boys," he said, "orphans eat free. Say, what I can't figure is why you're in such a hurry to find your uncle. He's gonna make rules and start telling you what to do. He'll probably whip you and make you stay in at night."

Judd's finger was in his mouth, wiggling a loose tooth. "I don't like our uncle," he said.

Danny whispered, "How can you say that?"

Smokey Joe laughed so hard, food spewed out of his mouth. "Well, even if your uncle's in Bodie, he sure won't jump for joy when two orphans knock on his door. Relax. Stick with us and we'll have some fun."

Danny felt confused. Suddenly finding family didn't seem so urgent. He was no longer hungry and he'd not had any beatings since the orphanage. It was true: Wherever Hank might be, he wouldn't know his sister had died or that his nephews were coming to live with him. Besides, he could be dead or in jail or too drunk to care.

What *was* the hurry?

Smokey Joe was a rough sort, someone his parents wouldn't have liked, but he wasn't all bad. And Buster looked like he needed another friend. If the four of them stayed together it wouldn't be so lonesome.

Smokey Joe dipped his finger into a pot of mustard, spread it on some roast beef, then wiped his hand on his shirt. "Another thing, O'Reilly, if you stick with us, we'll show you how to get rich. The miners here get four dollars and fifty cents for a whole day's work. That's twelve hours down in the hot, steamy earth. Buster and me, we got a way that's quicker and easier. Howdy, Stella."

All eyes turned to the girl opening the kitchen door. Her red hair was loose down her back and she wore a shawl over her dress, for it was cold outside. From a potato sack she pulled out two gray sweaters and handed them to Danny.

"My aunt Clara said I'm to watch over you and your little brother. I don't want to, but she said I must. Here."

He held the sweaters. "Thank you, miss, but don't worry about us, we don't need watchin' over. We are just fine." He gave a confident nod to Buster, then Smokey Joe. They now had friends, plenty of food, a place to stay. The last thing they needed was a girl to boss them around.

GOLD

Just before sunset Smokey Joe led Stella and the boys out the saloon's back door into a narrow alley. Lantern light was beginning to glow from windows and there was an aroma of wood smoke in the cold air. Danny was grateful for his sweater, even though the wool itched his neck and arms.

Smokey Joe pointed up Bonanza Street, which was lined with small dark shacks. Over each door hung a red lantern. "Whatever you O'Reillys do in Bodie, stay away, far away from there. Captain Billy said it's dangerous and what he says, goes. Two fellas got knifed there yesterday. Now come on."

Dim light marked the shops and houses of Chinatown. There was a strong odor of garlic and a sweet smell Danny couldn't identify. The windows were dingy and partially covered with strips of red paper that had Chinese writing on them. As they hurried by, they saw through an open door that there were men lying in bunks, smoking pipes.

Buster said, "These're opium dens. Don't ever go in. Never. Anyone who's a friend of Orientals will pick up their unsanitary habits and begin to stink like them. Even the Paiutes know to stay away from Chinatown."

They turned down King Street and cut behind Sam Chung's Store through another alley until they came to a low wooden fence, which they climbed over. Now they were behind Big Bertha's Saloon. Music and laughter could be heard through a broken window.

The sun's sinking behind the Sierra made the temperature drop so quickly that ice crusted along puddles of slops that had been tossed out windows. The children could see their breath as they stomped and rubbed their arms to keep warm.

Smokey Joe's match flared when he struck it against a stone. "Let's get to work," he said, lighting his cigar. "Stella, you go first this time."

Near the back step, he pulled aside a loose plank, revealing a hole big enough to crawl through. Stella knelt in the cold mud to wiggle under the floor, disappearing in the darkness. Buster followed.

Judd grabbed his brother's arm. "Don't make me go in there, please, Danny?"

"There's gold to be found," said Smokey Joe. "Don't you wanna see what falls out of the miners' pockets? It'll buy you a nice thick steak."

"No. I don't care." Judd continued to pinch his loose tooth, trying to twist it out.

Danny put his arm around his brother and hugged him protectively. At the mention of gold, he remembered they'd spent their last coin. With gold they could afford a room with a bed, instead of sleeping on Captain Billy's floor. With gold they'd be able to take a stage to Oregon, where Aunt Hattie would welcome them as sons.

"You wait right here," he said, "and I'll be back before you know it, all right, Judd?"

Under the saloon, it was cold as an icebox. Danny's knees and hands quickly grew numb as he crawled after the others. It was dark except for narrow strips of light slanting down through the floorboards, which thumped with dancers. Dust drifted onto his hair. He looked up to see boots shuffling and hopping to a polka. The accordian music was loud.

Smokey Joe pointed with the glowing red eye of his cigar. "Look for sparkle, Dan . . . see . . . like this." He scraped the dirt with his fingernail and held up a nugget the size of a mustard seed. He dropped it into

Danny's shirt pocket. "Here you go. That's worth maybe fifty cents. Take enough of 'em to the assayer, you could end up a millionaire."

Someone overhead cursed just as a coin dropped through the cracks. It landed in the dirt and rolled up to Danny's knee. Smokey Joe snatched it, turned it in the light, then clamped it between his teeth to test for softness. "Aha! Hard as a rock, boys, a twenty-dollar gold piece, straight from heaven."

Danny thought to snatch the coin back, but didn't want to fight. He turned away to begin his own search. He noticed Stella was dropping nuggets into her apron pocket.

"Aren't you going to fill up your potato bag?" he asked, crawling alongside her.

"Yes, I am, in a few minutes. You'll see."

Soon enough, Danny noticed moving shadows. He recognized the shapes, the same he'd seen every night in the orphanage. Rats. Dozens and dozens, darting from corner to corner, scurrying boldly in front of the children.

Stella grabbed a thick tail and flung the animal into her sack, twisting the top closed. Danny was shocked. "Why're you doing that?"

"Big Bertha pays us a nickel each if we drown 'em in those ponds below Standard Mill. Sometimes we make a dollar a night, just catching rats, that's not counting the gold flakes or coins we find. But you gotta be quick, like this."

She grabbed another tail and held it up. The rat was black and horrible, teeth bared, its four legs clawing the air. "You try, Danny. Hold 'em like this and they can't bite you."

He backed away. "No, thank you, miss. I'll just keep trying my luck with coins."

A TERRIBLE DISAPPOINTMENT

Winter suddenly was upon them.

The thermometer at Boone's General Store read twelve below zero, sometimes twenty below. Snow blew in great drifts, piling up against buildings two stories high. Children climbed out their upstairs windows to slide down to their yards where paths were tunneled to the outhouses.

Along Main Street, after the sidewalks were shoveled, there remained walls of ice fifteen feet high. Wagon ruts froze so that it was impossible for horses or carriages to cross street or alley. Instead, drivers parked at the edge of town to haul their goods in by sled.

Soon Danny had made six dollars in coins he found beneath saloons and dance halls. It seemed a fortune to him, but still it was not enough to move into a boardinghouse where rooms cost eight dollars a week, and meals were fifty cents if they wanted to eat at a table with a white cloth.

It was lonesome crawling under the buildings. It was dark and cold, but Danny liked the way Smokey Joe was trying to be his friend by sharing some of the big nuggets.

One night just before Christmas, Stella visited the Occidental Hotel. She proudly set her potato sack on the floor where it rippled like a large brown puddle. Because the ponds were frozen, she wanted to use one of the hotel's bathtubs to drown the rats. Judd's eyes grew wide.

"Rats?" he said.

"Ha," laughed Smokey Joe. "What a crybaby, you're afraid of everything. Why doncha grow up?"

Danny yanked the cigar from Joe's mouth. "Leave my brother alone or I'll break your arm."

"Oh, aren't you the one to talk, Mister Big Crybaby Himself. I know. I hear you every night . . . what a chump."

Danny swung his fist, but the boy ducked and threw his own punch, hitting Danny square in the stomach. As he fell he pulled Smokey Joe down in a headlock. Their new friendship forgotten, they rolled and kicked their way across the floor, unfortunately bumping into Stella's sack.

"Stop!" she screamed, but it was too late. The top, which had been folded closed, unfolded. Out darted a rat, followed by more, finally twenty-eight in all, large gray nervous things, scrambling to hide behind chairs, cupboards, and between dark cracks in the walls.

Stella reached down for Smokey Joe's neck and pulled him up by the collar. "You spoiled, selfish boy," she cried. "Look what you've done! They're everywhere." She grabbed his hair and started to slap him when Captain Billy stepped in to separate them.

"Now, now," he said. "This won't solve anything."

A woman's voice called out. It was Madame Mustache, hurrying in from another room, wearing a green satin dress with matching little shoes.

"Joe," she said, wagging her finger at the boy, "you stop your cur-sing, shame on you, shame. See how you've upset the lee-tle one? Come here, my darling, don't cry, everything will be all right." Madame settled herself in an armchair, pulling Judd into her lap. She kissed his cheek.

"Boys," she said, "a gentle-man came by earlier when you all were out, and he said he is Hen-ree Valentine. Captain Billy and I, we told this man that he must answer correctly one question, a question that only a relative of Daniel and Judd O'Reilly will be able to answer.

He works the night shift at Standard Mill so he will come by tomorrow morning first thing."

Upon hearing his uncle's name, Danny's heart sank.

Cold air from a broken attic window gusted downstairs where the boys lay curled together in a corner. There were seven children tonight, trying to stay warm. Though Captain Billy kept the fire blazing, the thermometer on the wall didn't rise above forty-six degrees.

Danny slept poorly because the rats were busy scratching inside the walls as they explored their new home. It also was hard to sleep because he felt confused. If this stranger really was their uncle, maybe their worries were over. On the other hand, Danny had begun to enjoy his independence, doing what he wanted, when he wanted. It was wonderful to finally have friends his own age. After all, he was twelve years old. He no longer needed adults to tell him what to do.

Finally dawn came. He was warming his hands around a cup of hot tea Captain Billy brought him when a miner in tall snowy boots walked in the door. His beard was frosted with ice.

"Howdy," he called, setting his hat on the billiard table. He smiled eagerly at each child. "I'm Henry Valentine. Any of you fellas answer to the name O'Reilly?"

Judd looked out from his blanket at the other boys, to see what he should do. He wanted this man to be his uncle, but he was silenced by the frown on Danny's face.

For this was the man they'd seen three months ago on Hidalgo Day, the man whose sweetheart was a Chinese girl.

CHRISTMAS EVE, 1878

As Danny walked over to the billiard table he searched the man's face. When he recognized his mother's blue-gray eyes and warm smile, Danny's troubled heart swelled with an affection he didn't understand. Suddenly he felt too shy to speak.

The man nodded toward Captain Billy and Madame Mustache. "Yesterday," he said to Danny, "these folks gave me some sad news about my sister and mentioned you want to ask me a question. Well, I am happy to tell you anything at all, so let's talk to each other, man to man."

Danny drew in a breath. "Well . . . our mother was born in an unusual place. Tell us where, also how she got her name."

The man slapped his knee and laughed. "Glad to. It's

a story I been told since I was a lad, so here it is: My sister — that's your mama — she was born in the summer of 1847, when Injuns was chasing their wagon train through Idaho Territory. My pa and the other men drove into the Snake River at Three Island Crossing, and well, seeing as how babies is born whenever they darn please, she was born right there between the middle and third islands, while the wagon was floatin' across. That's why they named her River. River Ann Valentine. As for me, I was born the next August in Oregon City, then two other brothers after me. That answer your question, fellas?"

Judd pushed aside his blanket and ran to throw his arms around the man's neck. "Uncle Hank," he said softly.

"That's me, sonny."

Confused, Danny waited. He wanted to rush into his uncle's strong arms. He wanted to pour out his grief, to be with someone who also had loved his mother. But the other boys were watching. They would make fun of him.

Smokey Joe broke the silence. "You still have doin's with that Chinese girl?" he asked. He was rolling a fresh cigar between his fingers, imitating the gamblers he'd seen at Madame's poker table.

51

"That's none of your business, now is it, young fellow? I'd like to have a word with my nephews, please. Alone."

"Why, yessir," said Captain Billy. His dark face beamed as he escorted them into his office, where a window looked out to the snowy street.

For several moments Uncle Hank watched a horse-drawn sleigh, which was being chased by a group of boys with snowballs. "Dan," he said in a quiet voice, "tell me about my sister, and your pa. What about little Susanna, did she . . . ?"

"She's going to be a nun!"

"No, she's not, Judd. She's only a baby." Danny explained why they left Susanna at St. Mary's, and how they wanted to return for her as soon as possible. He wondered aloud if it wouldn't be better for them to leave Bodie now and go live in Oregon with Hattie and Wade.

"We just had enough money to come here, Uncle Hank. . . ." Danny struggled to find words of apology, but wasn't sure what he was sorry for. He had managed to take care of himself and his brother for almost four months. He'd earned enough money to buy them each a coat, double-breasted wool like sailors wore, and he'd even bought himself a cap. They'd been eating at least one meal a day. They were doing just fine. But Danny now struggled against tears as he realized how much he missed his parents. It was his first Christmas without them.

Uncle Hank continued to gaze outside. Snow had begun to fall again, powdering the street and hitching posts. Large white flakes swirled with the wind. Another sleigh passed by, towing behind it two little pine trees that had been cut near Aurora. When Hank turned to face them, his eyes were wet.

"Fellas, I can't find words to tell you how sorry I am about you losing your folks. River was my only sister and I will miss her. I know she and your pa would want you boys to be taken in by someone who'd be good to you. Seems like God led you to the right place, because I will do just that."

Judd's grin showed off his missing top tooth. "Where's your house? Let's go."

Noticing Danny's silence, Uncle Hank put his hand on his shoulder. "Something wrong, son?"

How could Danny explain that the friends he'd made in town would tease him because of the Chinese girl? How could he tell this kind man he didn't need him after all?

Rather than hurt his uncle's feelings, Danny managed a smile and shook his hand. "I'm glad to see you, Uncle Hank."

They walked down Main to Green Street, then began climbing the slippery hill. Blowing snow stung their cheeks and made their ears numb. When they passed the schoolhouse, Danny remembered an early visit from Miss Polly, the teacher who had invited him to attend class, a conversation he'd forgotten until now. The further uphill they went, the more he felt out of breath from the altitude and cold air.

Uncle Hank stopped. He waved his mittened hand toward a cabin where stacks of firewood filled its porch. Once again his beard was white with frost.

"This here's home," he said. "Come on in, fellas, and we'll cook ourselves some breakfast."

A small iron stove was in the center of the room. Its smokestack poked up through the low ceiling, with a circle of white sky showing through. Snow was sifting down, melting into a puddle on the floor.

Wet clothes hung from rafters, giving off a stink. There were two bunk beds, a few stools, and a small square table where a cat sat licking its front paw, ignoring the boys. Picks and other tools were hooked to the walls; burlap sacks covered the windows.

"Five of us men call this home, and you fellas make it seven. Since we work different shifts we take turns sleeping in whatever bed's free. Don't be shy. Come in, come in."

Danny looked around the cluttered room and felt out of place. As his eyes grew accustomed to the dim light, he noticed someone in the corner, quietly plucking feathers from a dead goose.

It was the Chinese girl.

Her dark eyes watched the boys, then she bowed her head in a silent greeting.

Danny took his brother's hand. "Uncle Hank, I forgot something, I promised Captain Billy we'd help him. . . . It's Christmas Eve. . . ."

He bolted out into the blizzard. Tears froze on his cheeks as he pulled Judd along, slipping and running down the icy hill. Judd was hitting his arm, crying for him to let go.

"I want to stay with Uncle Hank! Where're we going, Dan?"

Danny hated himself. He didn't understand why he had just lied to his uncle or why he was running away from him. But as he tried to think things through, he kept hearing Smokey Joe's laugh. He remembered Buster's warnings to stay away from Chinatown. How could he and Judd live with someone who had a Chinese girlfriend?

The more he thought about his uncle, the more upset he felt. Danny didn't know what to do.

A THIEF ON SNOWSHOES

THE BLIZZARD ON CHRISTMAS EVE hit with such fierceness the lamps along Main Street blew out. Howling wind rattled doors and windows. Snow gusted into the Occidental Hotel every time someone opened the front door.

When the brothers came in without their uncle, Captain Billy stepped down from the Christmas tree he was decorating and looked at them with concern.

"Now, what on earth you two doing back here so quick? Did someone hurt you? Tell me, boys, something wrong?"

Danny squeezed his brother's hand hard enough to silence him. He didn't want anyone, especially Smokey Joe, to know the Chinese girl was at his uncle's cabin cooking for the five miners who lived there. And he didn't have the courage to decide if there was anything wrong with this. More than anything he didn't want his new friends to make fun of him.

"It's crowded, Captain Billy. We want to stay here where it's warmer."

Judd pulled away from Danny. "Liar," he whispered.

It stormed for twelve days. Snow drifted into the hotel through knotholes and cracks in the walls, then formed icy puddles on the floorboards. Several times Uncle Hank came to see his nephews and make sure they were warm. He didn't understand why Danny refused to live with him, nor did he know what to do about it. When the boys weren't watching, he gave Captain Billy his few spare coins to help pay for their food.

Finally the wind stopped. Danny heard shovels scraping snow from the plank sidewalks and, once again, the loud stamping of the mill. Snow was so deep that the windows facing Main Street were solid white, as if shades had been pulled down. Only from upstairs could the boys look out over the hills and stubble town. That is how they noticed a crowd gathered in front of the Wells Fargo office.

Wrapped in their coats, the brothers ran outside to join the other children who had climbed onto the slippery hitching rails. This way they were tall enough to hear what the men were saying: A stagecoach had been discovered halfway to Aurora, frozen in ice. The six horses were dead, as were the driver and two passengers. It had left Christmas Eve bound for Carson City, but apparently became trapped in heavy snow.

The loudest discussion, though, was not about the poor victims, but about a sack of missing gold, stolen by a thief on snowshoes.

Who? everyone asked. Had he ambushed the stage or had he been one of the passengers? And how could he have carried so much weight all by himself? Most mysterious was that the thief's tracks disappeared in front of a cave. The searchers went in as far as they could, but found no sign of the man or the gold.

Danny jumped down from the rail and swung underneath to tug on Smokey Joe's coat.

"Joe," he said, his breath making frost between them. "Let's get the others and meet at the Can-Can. We might be millionaires yet."

The kitchen was the saloon's warmest room. While the cook dished out bowls of stew for the children Danny explained his plan to them.

Stella sat on the bread table, listening. She wore wool leggings under her dress and a pair of heavy miner's boots that had belonged to her father. Her red hair was in one long braid over her shoulder, and her cheeks were bright.

"Why, if that isn't one of the stupidest things I've ever heard," she said. "Hiking through the snow in twenty-below-zero weather without telling anyone where we'll be? What are you thinking? If the cold won't kill us, the mountain lions will. Honest to pete, sometimes you fellas are thick as mules."

"Well, well," said Smokey Joe. "Look who thinks she's Queen Victoria. You're just scared."

"Scared nothing. Go ahead, try it. Gold never did a dead man a bit of good, that's what my aunt Clara says."

"Is that so?"

"Yes, that is so. And I'll tell you something else, smarty. Keeping our mouths shut may be the best thing we can do. Come spring, folks in town'll be so busy putting up new buildings, going deeper into the mines, and playing the stock market they'll likely forget about the thief on snowshoes, and we'll have the search all to ourselves."

Danny was silent. He wanted to smack Stella for being so bossy, but she was probably right. This made him maddest of all.

THE LONG WINTER

DANNY HAD NEVER experienced such a rough winter. Even Captain Billy said it was the worst in memory. The tin cup hanging by the water barrel outside was dented from children using it to break the ice.

"Never seen s'much snow in all the years I been out West, no sir." He worked hard to keep the hotel warm for his customers, but mostly for the children. Every other week he washed their blankets and clothes, then strung ropes across the lobby so he could hang things to dry. Men wanting to play pool did so by ducking under a shirt here, a pair of knickers there.

Captain Billy, who'd lost his own parents at a young age, had a soft heart for the orphans. He saw to it that they had a warm cup of soup before going to bed, and after they were asleep the old man crept downstairs to tuck them in. For breakfast he gave them buttered bread and, when it was available, cocoa. He scolded the boys for fighting, and worried when they stayed out too late. As they left each morning to explore town he said, "You fellas, stay warm now, hear?"

Usually Madame Mustache was there, too, with a hot biscuit to tuck in each of their pockets. She often reminded them that school was a good place for smart boys like them to be.

It was Captain Billy who searched the lumberyards for planks of wood ten feet long and four inches wide, wood that was warped at the ends from being left out in the snow. He brought them into the lobby, lay them across the tops of chairs, then drilled holes in the middle of the planks. At his direction, Madame Mustache hurried down to the saddlemaker where she bought strips of leather and some tiny silver buckles. These she wove into the wood to form a type of stirrup. When finished, they lay the planks on the floor.

"Judd, stand here," said Captain Billy, lifting the small boy so his feet slipped into the straps, which Madame buckled tight. Next he sawed off the handle to one of his brooms and gave it to Judd.

"Get yourself out onto the snow, my friend, and push yourself along like you's in a boat. Couple years ago some Norwegians stayed here and made these snowshoes for themselves and, mercy, they slid all over these hills. One fella even made it all the way to Mammoth City in just a couple days."

Captain Billy crafted several pairs, making sure the front tips curved upward. This way the shoes would glide over the snow instead of digging into it.

With the skis over their shoulders, the orphans hiked up Green Street, past the schoolhouse, then up past Uncle Hank's cabin. From the top of the bluff the view was spectacular. Snow covered the hills in every direction, as if a fine downy quilt had been carefully spread out. To the west were the Sierra's jagged peaks, to the south the gray oval of Mono Lake.

"Well, who wants to go first?" asked Smokey Joe.

Danny looked down the hill. It was much steeper from up here, and a long way to the bottom. He shivered with cold as the wind cut through his thin layer of clothes and stung his face and bare hands. What he really wanted to do was take the skis off and walk with Judd back down to the Occidental Hotel, then soak himself in a nice, hot, steamy bath.

Smokey Joe saw him hesitate. "Chicken," he said.

"Am not."

"Then prove it. I dare you, O'Reilly."

Danny pushed himself off with Judd's pole, hurling himself full speed downhill. When he caught his breath from the sudden rush of of icy air, he realized he hadn't given thought to how he would stop.

With a whoosh he flew across Wood Street, then still gaining speed, a few seconds later he crossed Main, miraculously sliding between two sleighs piled high with firewood. The customers at Boone's General Store looked out the window to see a quick spray of snow as Danny sailed by. He passed Mills Street, then Park Street where a ridge in the intersection launched him ten feet into the air.

Afraid he'd hit the upcoming livery stable he pulled his knees to his chest, ducked his chin, and rolled onto his side, landing hard in a pile of hay. The force of his fall snapped off his skis and knocked him out. His cap landed in the corral.

"Well, I'll be," said Big Bertha who had been pouring slops into the hog pen next door. She marched over to Danny, bent down to get a good look at him, then patted his cheek. "Wake up, boy. You hurt?"

A shout pierced the cold air. "Here comes another one!"

Big Bertha looked up to see a small dark object barreling down the hill. It was Buster.

"Sit down!" folks along the sidewalk began shouting to him. It looked like Buster was trying to sit, but he was going too fast. When he slid into Main Street, he struck the rear wheel of a laundry cart.

A stunned crowd gathered around him. "Good Lord, his neck's broke," someone said.

Shouting men hurried up the snowy hill, waving their arms so the other children wouldn't take off. Uncle Hank heard the screams and ran out of his cabin. In one swoop he lifted Judd, unbuckled his skis, and carried him out of danger. Stella and three of the other boys glared at Smokey Joe before turning their backs on him and beginning their hike downhill.

In the lobby that night Captain Billy rocked with grief. "That poor chile," he kept saying. "Why did I let you boys go out, oh, why? I thought you would jess go slidin' around the streets like I say, not down a mountain, mercy. That poor chile, at least now he's in heaven with his mammy and pap." Captain Billy was so brokenhearted he sawed the skis into pieces, then threw them in the fire.

A doctor came to bandage Danny's ribs and to sew up a deep cut on his arm. He took a bottle of laudanum from his black bag and uncorked it so Danny could have a few sips. Soon he was drowsy. His last thought before sleep took him was how grateful he was that Uncle Hank had stopped Judd in time.

A mule pulled the sled with Buster's coffin out of town and up the cold slope to the cemetery. That morning three blasts of dynamite had carved his grave out of the frozen earth. It was snowing as a small gathering of friends watched the burial.

Madame Mustache and Captain Billy wept quietly. Stella and her aunt were there, so was Smokey Joe, his eyes cast down. Uncle Hank stood by Judd with his arm around him, the Chinese girl at his side. Danny wondered why he'd brought her. What right did she have to come to an American funeral?

THE AMERICAN

DANNY MISSED BUSTER and felt responsible for his death. He was ashamed that he'd accepted Smokey Joe's dare, and that he'd put his little brother in danger. How foolish he'd been. How sorry he was that Buster had been killed.

He consoled himself by walking through town every morning. After making sure Judd was safe with Captain Billy, he would scuff along the board sidewalks, looking in windows and making friends with shopkeepers. Soon he was delivering groceries for City Market to earn nickel tips. He swept floors at the photographer's studio and the tin shop. And then, for a free lunch, he helped Stella clear tables at her aunt Clara's boarding-house.

Danny enjoyed his days doing what he wanted. In February when Miss Polly again visited him and the other orphans, she pleaded with them to attend school. They would be safe and busy, no more accidents.

But Danny told her, "Thank you very much, but Judd and I prefer not to go to school at present." He knew it would be torture to sit at a desk for hours on end.

Why only yesterday the boys had enjoyed staying up all night watching fireworks for Chinese New Year. And their next midnight adventure was to spy on the undertaker to see if it was true that he dug up graves. Rumor was he dumped the bodies down an old mine shaft, then resold the coffins as new. If the boys were up all night, how could they go to school the next day?

Also, Danny reasoned, there were card games to learn and soon it would be warm enough to explore under the saloons again. And Smokey Joe had promised he'd take them down into one of the mines. No, ma'am, there was no time for school.

By early May there were still mounds of snow in the shade of buildings. The white hills were spotted with dirt. As snow in the mountain passes began to melt, more wagons were able to make it into the swampy streets of Bodie.

This meant that fresh produce was delivered from the farms and orchards at lower elevations. Also, nearly thirty new people arrived every day, hoping to find their fortunes. They came from all over America and Europe. They opened shops, cafes, and bakeries; they built shacks off Main Street, and hired on as dancers, chefs, and miners. Some lost all their money their first afternoon in gambling parlors; others got rich overnight. Everyone read with excitement the signs that Wells Fargo posted around town: REWARD — $3,000 FOR RETURN OF GOLD STOLEN CHRISTMAS EVE 1878.

Danny was disappointed that people had not forgotten about the lost gold because he still planned to find it himself. With money he'd be able to afford a stagecoach to take them to Oregon, then he could buy a horse or whatever else he and Judd wanted. He was tired of working so hard for a nickel here and a dime there.

Often he stopped at the Magnolia Saloon to have a steak at the chop stand. He would pull up a stool near Madame Mustache's table and, balancing his plate on his knee, watch her run the faro game. She would wink at him, but otherwise say nothing. Cigar smoke was heavy in the room. Swiftly, she would deal cards to men seated in a half-circle around her. A small gold bracelet on her wrist clicked every time her hand swept against the wood.

"Gentle-men, place your bets." Her green eyes studied each player to make sure he wouldn't cheat, then she would kick one of them under the table. "You cuss one more time, I throw you out."

One afternoon during a game of *vingt-et-un* she called to Danny, "Stand up. Here comes your un-cull. Show him respect or I scold you."

Uncle Hank removed his hat and nodded to Madame. When he saw Danny, his face broke into a wide smile. "There you are. Come on, I have a few surprises."

Danny set his plate and knife on the bar, then followed him out to the cold sunshine. "Where're we going?" he asked.

"You'll see." As they walked, he put his arm on Danny's shoulder. "I have three days off on account I traded schedules and I want to show my nephews something interesting. Here we are."

They came to Tuolumne Livery Stable where a blacksmith wearing a long, leather apron held the halters of two horses hitched to a wagon. Judd was up on the seat, eager to go. Sitting on a blanket in back was the Chinese girl. When Danny realized she was coming, too, he turned away.

"I can't go," he said.

"Please, Dan. Hop in. I'd like you to meet Lu-Chen. Lu, this is my other nephew. I'm sorry it took me so long to introduce you all. Guess I've been living in the wilds too long."

"Hello," she said.

Danny nodded to her, but refused to smile.

He glanced down the street to make sure none of his friends were watching. The eager look on his uncle's face and Judd's happy chatter convinced him to go. He boosted himself up and settled between some boxes of food and a rolled-up tent. To make sure no one saw him he slid down and pulled a blanket over his head.

They rode out of town, through a field where a group of boys was playing baseball. The horses pulled up a hill, then along a ridge. The wind was cold up here. Danny peeked out from his blanket and when he saw they were on the desolate Cottonwood Trail leading to Mono Lake, he sat up.

Lu-Chen smiled and held out an orange for him. How delicious it looked.

"No, thanks."

"Why don't you like me?" she asked in perfect English.

"What?" He'd heard her, but was so surprised she didn't have an accent, he didn't know what to say.

"Well, every time you see me, you make a face. It makes your uncle sad."

Danny's mouth was open as he tried to think. He looked at her dark eyes, her wide cheeks, her long black hair.

"But you sound like an American," he said.

"Daniel, I am an American."

MONO LAKE

WIND WHIPPED ACROSS THE GRAY LAKE, stirring up foamy waves. Danny stared in wonder at the shoreline where in places there stood towerlike formations that were also gray. They reminded him of the sand castles he and Judd used to dribble with mud, only these were taller than he was. Across the bay a group of Paiutes stood in the shallow water, fishing with nets.

Uncle Hank smiled at his nephews. "This lake is a crater of an old volcano," he said. "It's full of briny fish and shrimp that the Indians love to eat. Come on, fellas, lift a hand, we'll camp here tonight. Tomorrow, your surprises."

The next morning Uncle Hank uncovered a rowboat in the reeds that had been left for him by a rancher. Lu-Chen filled their canteens in a nearby stream, then she packed them into the boat with three empty baskets.

There were two islands in the lake. While Uncle Hank rowed them to the largest, flocks of seagulls circled overhead.

Judd became excited. "Like the harbor, remember, Danny?"

"That's right, my boy," Uncle Hank said, pointing west. "The ocean's yonder, one hundred miles. Every spring the gulls come to these islands to nest — beats me why they come all this way, but they do, and their eggs have provided many a hearty breakfast. We sell them in camp for a dollar-fifty a dozen. Here we are." Uncle Hank jumped into the shallow water and held the bow so Lu-Chen could step onto the beach.

"Race me, Danny," Judd cried as he leaped out. But this island was not like the ones near San Francisco for with each step Judd sank to his knees. The beach was gray with ash and small pumice stones. He scooped up a handful and threw them into the water. The stones were as light as popcorn and floated for a few moments before sinking.

Lu-Chen carried one of her baskets up a small hill where black rock formed a protective barrier from the wind. Several gulls rose from their nests with a noisy complaint. She filled the basket with pumice then carefully layered the eggs inside. Danny watched, but didn't offer to help. He didn't like eggs and he didn't like her.

He followed Uncle Hank up to a ridge that was ankle-deep in ash. From there they could see the lake spread out for miles, a wilderness of wind and distant mountains. The air was clouded with seagulls, wheeling and crying.

Their cries reminded Danny of fishing with his father from the wharf. A tightness came to his throat. He took a deep breath and struggled not to cry. Wiping his face with his sleeve he looked at his uncle. His wavy, brown hair was swept back from his forehead, *just like Mother's,* thought Danny . . . the same open smile, the same eyes.

"Well, Dan," said Uncle Hank. "Here's one of your surprises: Did you ever think you'd be standing on top of a volcano? Lookee there." He pointed to a crevice where jets of steam rose from the hardened black lava.

"Once me and some fellas boiled our eggs right there in that hot pool. Say, just look at that brother of yours," he laughed. Judd was still throwing pumice into the air, this time trying to hit the gulls who hovered overhead like kites.

"My, my, I used to do that when I was a boy, throw rocks at things. Follow me, Dan, there's another surprise yonder." Uncle Hank sat on the ridge and slid down the hill, his feet plowing up gray dust. He reached the shore in a run and dove into the water.

When he came up for a breath, he cried, "Come on in, but whatever you do, keep your eyes closed!"

Danny took off his cap, then eased himself into the small waves. The water was cold and it felt soapy. He watched his uncle undress himself, then swish his trousers and blue shirt through the water. To Danny's amazement, foamy bubbles appeared.

"Best laundry there is," Uncle Hank yelled above the splashing. "Dunk yourself, boy, and scrub your hair, but do not open your eyes, the alkali will sting like crazy."

The last thing Danny wanted to do was take a bath, especially with Lu-Chen nearby. So he sat in the shallows and tilted his head back. Ice-cold water dripped down his neck. Rubbing his scalp, suds foamed up high as a hat, which gave him the idea to wash his clothes while wearing them.

While Danny scrubbed at his wet sleeves and pant legs, Uncle Hank tossed his own clothes onto the beach then rolled over to swim on his back. He was still wearing his skivvies.

"Try it, Dan, this lake's saltier than the ocean, so you float like a boat. Yippee!"

Danny was surprised to see his uncle have fun, almost as if he were still a boy himself. Soon Judd was there, too, wading up to his knees. Uncle Hank took his arms and playfully pulled him through the water, careful not to splash the boy's eyes. The water was so cold that when Judd began shivering Uncle Hank carried him to shore. He helped him undress, then spread their shirts and trousers over a boulder to dry. Danny kept his wet clothes on.

The brothers lay in the warm sun. The sound of waves lapping on the beach and the cry of seagulls was so familiar, so comforting, the boys soon fell into a deep sleep. When Danny woke three hours later, his clothes had dried, but he was cold. There was wind off the lake and the sun was low in the sky, almost touching the peaks of the Sierra. On the far side of the shore a herd of mule deer drank from a freshwater creek.

Uncle Hank was helping Lu-Chen carry her baskets of eggs to the boat. He brought a canteen to Danny, then shook out Judd's clothes so he could dress. Danny looked at his uncle's sunburned face. His hair was tangled from the wind and his beard seemed red from the setting sun. He was a rugged man, almost handsome, thought Danny. Will I look like him? he wondered.

"There's one last surprise, Dan, and I believe you are man enough to understand." Uncle Hank glanced toward the shore where breaking waves pushed at their boat. The lake looked like a stormy sea.

Danny was beginning to feel nervous. "What is it, Uncle?"

After a moment Uncle Hank said, "Lu-Chen and I are to be married."

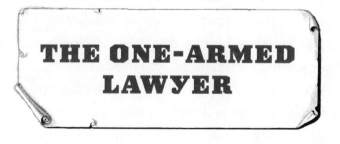

THE ONE-ARMED LAWYER

THEY CAMPED A SECOND NIGHT on the windswept shore of Mono Lake. Danny tucked an extra blanket around his brother, then rolled on his back to watch the stars. He hadn't spoken to his uncle all evening, nor did he the next day.

He was ashamed that out of all the men in Bodie who might dare to marry a Chinese girl, it would be his very own uncle. *Why?* Not only was it against the law, it just wasn't right. Soon Smokey Joe and the others would find out and there would be no end to their ridicule.

In town Danny busied himself with looking after Judd in the mornings, then went to his various jobs. The butcher at City Market gave him an armful of groceries to deliver to the new lawyer in town, Pat Reddy, the name and address written in charcoal on the sack.

Mud splashed Danny's legs as he crossed Main then

turned down Union Street. He was careful not to let the mobs of people bump him, for he didn't want the bag to rip. He grew hungry from the delicious aroma of fresh-ground coffee, bread, and chocolate.

A cottage on Prospect Place was crowded with men carrying in crates and satchels from a wagon parked in front. Danny stood by the porch and called, "Mr. Reddy, please?"

The wagon driver walked through a wide puddle over to Danny. He was wearing a Confederate cap and a gray soldier's coat, and his pants were stained with mud. The handle of a knife stuck out the top of his boot.

"What d'you want, boy?" he said, reaching into the grocery sack. His dirty hand pulled out a chunk of bread, which he shoved into his mouth.

"Hey!" cried Danny, backing away. "That's not for you."

"Oh, yeah? I ain't et since Mammoth City. Come here."

Danny turned to run up the steps, but the man's hand on his shoulder held him. His breath stank of rotten eggs. "You trying to tell me what to do, boy?"

"No, sir, I'm just looking for Mr. Reddy."

When the man's grip tightened, Danny gasped in pain and made a quick decision. Holding the sack in his right arm, he reached up with his left hand and pulled the man's beard, at the same time kicking him as hard as he could in the thigh. This so surprised the old soldier that he let go and Danny ran into the house.

A tall man caught him. "Well, well," he said. "I could use a lad like you. What's your name?"

"Danny O'Reilly, sir."

"Aha, a fellow Irishman, God bless ye. I'm the one you seek, Patrick Reddy, Attorney-at-Law, formerly of Independence, California, here to defend the underdog of Bodie. Come in, lad, set the bag there."

The man pointed to a table against the parlor window. He had bushy red hair with thick sideburns and a handlebar mustache. Danny was surprised to see the man was missing an arm.

"Ah, don't mind this, lad," Reddy said. "Lost it in a shootout, I did, in the wild streets of Virginia City, but it has been a blessing in disguise. Here ye go." From his vest pocket he pulled out a silver dollar and slipped it into Danny's palm.

When Danny's eyes grew wide, the man said, "Ye deserve it, lad. I can see you're a hard worker. Come to my office tomorrow, second floor of the Molinelli Building upstairs from their saloon. I'll need help unpacking these books and other such."

For a moment Danny was speechless. *A real silver dol-*

lar. "Thanks, mister!" He dashed outside but the wagon driver stopped him on the porch. He pulled his knife from his boot and pointed it at Danny.

"You're coming with me, boy."

But Danny felt so happy he suddenly wasn't afraid. He backed up to the railing, swung his legs to the other side, then jumped.

"Oh, no, I'm not going with you." Danny ran to the corner where he disappeared into the crowds of Union Street.

A NEW JOB

THE OPENED WINDOWS of Pat Reddy's office looked down onto Main Street. The noise of wagons and horses and crowds of people reminded Danny so much of San Francisco he sometimes forgot he was in a mining camp high in the mountains.

For several days he stepped up and down a ladder in the law library, to put away books that were so heavy he could carry just two at a time. Because the hardwood floors had no carpets, Danny could see through the knotholes down to Molinelli's Saloon where the sounds of gamblers often drowned out the piano music.

Skylights brought sunshine into the law office, and ceiling fans stirred the air that was heavy with odors from the street below. Now with the weather warmer Danny could smell manure, garbage, and the contents of chamber pots that people poured out their windows.

Mr. Reddy's desk was solid oak with a rolled top; its cubbyholes were stuffed with papers and envelopes, and there were many tiny drawers barely big enough to hide a key. Lined against the office walls were crates of legal documents and ledgers, and tall oak file cabinets. The waiting area had a spittoon and one chair.

Such was Pat Reddy's reputation that even before he hung out his shingle, people — mostly poor — began coming for advice. Danny could hear them walking up the stairs: the heavy steps of miners, the clicking shoes of dance hall girls; Chinese laundry men came quietly in their silk slippers. He did not see any Indians.

Danny made himself busy by dusting furniture, filing papers, mopping, anything to earn his new salary, and anything to be able to observe the clients and hear their interesting stories. He enjoyed Sheriff Kirgan's daily visits because he brought the latest news of Chinatown and troublemakers who'd landed in jail the night before. The best news, though, came one summer morning when Danny was polishing the hat rack.

Sheriff Kirgan gave Danny a friendly pat on the shoulder, then seated himself in the waiting area, swiveling the chair around so he could prop his boots on the windowsill. His brass star reflected sunlight as he lit a cigar.

"Pat," he said, "it's time to draw up papers to cancel the reward money for that stolen gold. The thief has either gambled the coins away by now or snowshoed up to Alaska, so we've called off the search. I'll be telegraphing Wells Fargo in Carson City this afternoon."

When Danny reported this to his friends, they smiled at each other. Without a reward folks would stop looking. Now the children could have the hunt all to themselves.

Every morning before sunrise, Danny folded his blanket, ate a bowl of hot porridge that Madame Mustache cooked for him, put on his cap, then walked two blocks to City Market. He swept the sidewalk, then delivered groceries to some of the cafes in time for them to serve breakfast. For this he earned thirty-five cents a day. At nine o'clock he reported to Mr. Reddy. Sometimes the lawyer just asked him to listen while he practiced a speech or legal arguments, waving his one arm for emphasis. When he dismissed Danny at noon, he always slipped a silver dollar into his palm.

"Be careful out there, laddie," he said as he opened the door for him.

This is when Danny's real work began.

He hurried back to the Occidental Hotel. First he hid his money pouch in the kitchen beneath the pantry's floorboards, then he ate a quick lunch with Judd and Smokey Joe. Afterward the boys headed outside, walking along the crowded sidewalks to Clara's Boardinghouse where Stella waited for them. From there the four wandered into the hills at the edge of town, in search of clues to the lost treasure.

They didn't know what they were looking for, but with a cheerfulness known only to children they searched with high hopes.

The afternoons were hot. Because of the altitude their cheeks and hands became dark red with sunburn. Their shoes filled with sand, which caused blisters on the soles of their feet, and with just one canteen between them they were soon thirsty.

Stella scolded her friends not look under stones and rotted timbers. Black widows and scorpions made nests in such places and she knew boys liked to poke sticks at them. If they were to find the gold before anyone else, they could waste no time experimenting with bugs. Snakes were another problem. The children were careful where they stepped because sometimes a diamondback rattler would be napping in the middle of a trail.

One afternoon when dark gray clouds filled the sky

and thunder rumbled overhead, Stella saw something shiny under a ledge.

"Over there, look!" she cried.

As heavy raindrops began pelting them, they ran for cover under an outcropping of rocks, which turned out to be an entrance to a mine. They saw that the tunnel was full of dirt, as if the roof had caved in. Stella pointed to what had caught her eye: It was a silver buckle on a boot and next to it was some calico cloth.

The children kneeled and started digging with their hands, but when a sudden foul odor made their eyes sting, they backed away in horror. There in front of them was a partially exposed body, apparently a woman's because of the high-heeled boot and calico dress.

Stella and the boys looked at each other. What would a lady be doing near a mine shaft?

Moments later when they noticed a pair of snowshoes wedged under a rock, a hush fell over the children. One by one they sat down on the floor of the cave, unable to speak, for such a discovery was too great for words.

Finally Danny cleared his throat. "So the thief was a lady?" he said. "Is it possible the gold is here, too?"

Danny was bothered that they were so close to a dead body, but he didn't say so. It was hard not to think of his own mother who was so recently in the grave. At this memory he looked at Judd with tenderness, then leaned forward to brush dirt from the boy's cheek.

While the children puzzled over this mystery, they sat in the warm protection of the cave, listening to the rain hiss as it touched the dry earth. Lightning struck the horizon, followed by a crack of thunder. They could see out across the hills where the muddy road cut through the mountains from Aurora. A pack train of burros hauling firewood toward Bodie was far enough away that the rain put silence between them and the Chinese who were herding the animals.

The children felt safely hidden and, most importantly, they felt their secret was safe.

As they watched the storm, Danny grew nervous. Rainclouds blackened the sky and the air was growing cold. He remembered Uncle Hank's warning about high-Sierra weather: Even though it was summer, the air temperature could drop to freezing in minutes. Snowstorms in June were common in Bodie.

"We'd better get going," he said. "We can come back tomorrow."

Stella tore off a piece of the dress. While she held it between her fingers, trying to understand what had happened to the poor woman, the boys quickly buried the snowshoes and the boot with the silver buckle.

TREASURE HUNT

THE NEXT DAY Danny and his friends returned to the cave, but somehow all the rocks had been removed and now there were rail tracks leading into the side of the mountain. Smokey Joe threw his cigar into the dark tunnel.

"I can't believe we're so stupid," he yelled, his voice echoing far away. "This isn't it. We're lost. All the hills around here look alike; all the caves look alike. Come on, let's get outa here."

It took three weeks for the children to retrace their steps. When they finally found their abandoned mine, they decided to mark the spot so they'd never get lost again. Smokey Joe pulled from his shirt pocket a roll of red twine that he'd bought in Chinatown. With their penknives the boys cut pieces two inches long, then planted the pieces in the dirt so just the red tips showed. They made a trail down toward the road, but stopped behind a ledge so no travelers would notice.

"If we didn't know what we were looking for, we wouldn't know what we're looking at," said Danny, pleased at their cleverness. Soon they'd be rich as bankers. Danny knew the first thing he'd buy would be tickets back to San Francisco where he and Judd would get baby Susanna, then tickets for Oregon. The more he thought about this the more excited he felt: He couldn't wait to leave Bodie. Uncle Hank could marry the Chinese girl and it wouldn't bother him a bit.

Every day they returned to their trail of red string, careful to start out on different paths each time, so no one would get suspicious. For this reason they didn't carry shovels, but instead brought along pie tins for digging, hidden inside their shirts. When other children asked if they could come, too, Stella said, "Of course you may. We're going to study clouds from the top of Miner's Bluff."

It took just one brisk hike, straight uphill, for the others to decide they could see clouds just fine from Bodie Creek, where it was much more fun to fish for brookies. "I feel bad for lying," Stella told Danny, "but I didn't know how else to keep our secret."

Each afternoon the four children knelt in their cave

and used their hands and pie tins to cut into the dirt, careful not to uncover the woman's body. Judd often stopped because he was tired. His arms were scraped and dusty. He didn't understand what he was looking for or why, but he wanted to please his brother so after a few moments' rest, he kept digging. When he saw what looked like a pile of white poker chips, he scooped up a handful.

"Hey, Danny, look," he cried.

Stella took one of the chips, spit on it, then rubbed it with the hem of her dress. Holding up a twenty-dollar gold piece she said. "Fellas, we're rich."

Danny was stunned. Could this really be the lost gold? They began digging feverishly. But after fifteen minutes they ran into solid rock, a boulder too heavy to move.

They sat against the wall of the cave, exhausted. Their hands were bloodied and they'd uncovered only eight coins, which, divided evenly, meant two coins each. Surely there were more, for sticking out from underneath the boulder was part of a canvas bag. Just the faded black letters *A-R-G-O* could be seen.

"It *is* the Wells Fargo money," Stella said. "But how can we get to it?"

Smokey Joe struck a match to light his cigar. Between clenched teeth he said, "Dynamite."

"Are you crazy?" said Danny. "That'll bring the whole town."

"Not if we do it on the Fourth of July. Danny m'boy, the Civil War Veterans shoot off so many cannons it sounds like the Battle of Gettysburg. That and all the firecrackers, no one'll hear a peep out of us."

Danny thought about this. He wasn't going to say it, but dynamite scared him. He'd seen the mangled bodies after an explosion the month before in the Buttermilk Mine. Ever since Buster's ski accident Danny vowed he'd never again put his brother in danger. And something else bothered him.

"What about the lady?" he said, pointing to the pile of rocks that covered her body. "She should have a proper burial even if she was a thief."

Smokey Joe cursed. "You are such a chump, O'Reilly. Who cares? She's dead. Besides, she was probably just one of those saloon girls."

"Wait," said Stella. "I agree. We need to tell someone about her, someone we can trust."

"Ah, come on, you two, there ain't a soul in this crummy camp —"

Danny held up his hand. "Yes, there is."

That afternoon Danny and Stella found Madame Mustache in the cemetery on the north side of town.

She was kneeling at Buster's grave, trying to plant flowers from wild onions and a small sagebrush. Its buds left yellow powder on her black dress and black sleeves, but she didn't seem to notice. Tears stained her face.

"Such a sweet, sweet boy . . ." she said before sobs consumed her. When she felt Stella at her side, she put her arms around the girl and reached up to hold Danny's hand. "Oh, how I adore you sweet children," she told them.

The three walked down the windswept hill to the road that led into town. By the time they reached the Magnolia Saloon where Madame was to work the faro tables, they had told her about the dead woman, leaving out the part about the gold.

"Maybe you can recognize her by her dress," Stella said, holding up the torn piece. "Surely she had family or someone who cared about her."

Madame nodded sadly. The calico matched a dress worn by her friend Lilly, a dancer at the Can-Can. Now Madame understood why no one had seen Lilly since the Christmas blizzard.

A TERRIFIC EXPLOSION

THE WOMAN'S BURIAL took place the next night, by the light of a half-moon. Captain Billy was brought into the secret, at least part of it, for he was strong and he asked no questions. Together he, Danny, and Smokey Joe wrapped the body in a sheet and carried it to an abandoned mine shaft on the dark side of the hill.

Madame Mustache followed, holding Judd's hand and Stella's. Big Bertha came, too, because she had known Lilly well.

In the shadowy moonlight Madame spoke kindly of her friend. Why she died in the lonely cave, she didn't know, nor did she ask the children what they'd been doing up there. She did know that shame was connected to the death and she did not want to shame her friend further with a public funeral in town.

After Captain Billy said a prayer, he and the boys rolled the body into the shaft, then swept in enough rocks to cover it. Thereafter, he, Madame, and Big Bertha never spoke of this night.

In preparation for the Fourth of July, small cottonwood trees were brought in from Mammoth City and planted in buckets along Main Street. Banners hung from balconies and American flags flew from upstairs windows.

Madame Mustache served fresh strawberries to the children for breakfast, brought in the day before from a farm in Mono Valley. Danny wanted to tell her about the gold because he thought a grown-up should know. Somewhere in his memory were his mother's words: *If you find something that's been lost, try to find its owner.*

When he mentioned this to the others, Smokey Joe said, "O'Reilly, if you breathe a word of this I will cut your throat and dump your body in Miss Lilly's grave."

For now, Danny found it easier to go along with Smokey Joe than to fight him, but one thing he would not back down on was this: He would keep his brother safe — Judd was to stay with Captain Billy so he could watch the parade and baseball games.

"Have fun today, my sweet ones," Madame said as

Smokey Joe and Danny hurried through the lobby and out the door. She held Judd, who was waving good-bye with a small American flag, on her lap.

The boys met Stella at Marco's Emporium. When they requested a small keg of blasting powder and a length of fuse three feet long, Mr. Marco smiled. He rang up their purchase on his silver-plated register and said, "Here y'go, kids. What's Fourth of July without a little noise? That's my motto."

The children dug a hole under the boulder. After pouring in the dynamite, they buried one end of the fuse with it, then stomped dirt on top. They sat in the cave, waiting, the fuse stretched out beside them like a pet snake.

Finally, at twelve o'clock noon, the old soldiers in town began firing their cannons.

Smokey Joe jumped up. "This is it, let's go!" He pressed the burning end of his cigar to the fuse until it began to sizzle.

"Run for it!" Danny yelled. He grabbed Stella's hand and dragged her from the cave, Smokey Joe close behind. They slid downhill, skinning their knees and hands as they tried to keep from falling. In a moment they rounded a bluff and dove behind a wall of rock. Before they could cover their heads an explosion shattered with such force that the ground shook and a ledge above them broke off, narrowly missing their legs as it tumbled down to the road.

Dirt and pebbles rained on them, then something else that made Danny feel sick inside.

A fine, yellow dust was drifting onto their shoulders and outstretched palms. "Our gold," he whispered.

They stood up and cautiously walked around the bluff where they'd be able to see their cave. The opening was now three times as wide and most of the roof, which actually was the side of the mountain, had been blown off. The boulder was no longer there.

And neither was the gold.

Danny turned to Smokey Joe, yanked the soggy cigar out of his mouth, and crushed it in his trembling hand.

"Smokey Joe," he said, "I will never again let you tell me what to do."

ANOTHER THIEF

Danny lay wrapped in his blanket under the billiard table. It was seven o'clock in the morning and even though the other orphans were already eating breakfast he didn't want to get up.

He was furious with himself for listening to Smokey Joe. If only he'd told Madame and Captain Billy about the gold then maybe it could have been safely rescued. Maybe Wells Fargo would have given a reward after all. His and Judd's two coins seemed a fortune to him, but $80 still was not enough to get to Oregon.

While he lay there, he watched the comings and goings of hotel patrons and other customers. When he saw someone in tall muddy boots with a knife sheathed to the leg, Danny felt a nervous turn in his stomach. He leaned out from under the table to see the man's face and quickly ducked back.

It was the wagon driver he'd run into at Mr. Reddy's house the day he delivered groceries. Maybe the man had forgotten about him, but Danny wasn't taking chances. He crawled out the other side and hurried into the parlor where Smokey Joe was sweeping the floor.

"Sure, I saw him before," he told Danny. "I thought you knew him because a couple days ago he said he had a surprise for you."

Puzzled, Danny peeked around the corner where he could see Captain Billy wiping down the bar. Madame was nearby, showing Judd how to carefully slice an apple. The kitchen was behind them. Danny saw the wagon driver pass by the stove, then go into the pantry. Danny moved closer.

A moment later the man stepped out of the pantry and put something in his pocket. Danny gasped when he realized it was his and Judd's money pouch.

"Hey!" Danny yelled, rushing toward him.

"Well, well, if it ain't the little rich boy himself. Scram, kid."

"I worked hard for that money," Danny cried. He ducked his head and tackled the man's legs, knocking him to the floor.

Suddenly Judd was there, too, and with a swiftness that surprised even himself he reached down with his small hands and pulled the knife out of the boot. Judd pointed the blade at the man.

"Mister, if you don't give us back our money I'm going to cut your eyeballs out."

The man was so startled he stopped struggling for a moment, long enough for Danny to twist the thief's arms behind his back. Meanwhile, Madame Mustache slipped her blue silk scarf from her neck and tied his wrists together.

The pouch had fallen and spilled its coins. Captain Billy bent down to scoop them up while calling over his shoulder to Smokey Joe.

"Run and get Sheriff Kirgan quick as y'can, that's my boy. Mister, you ought to be 'shamed of yourself, stealing from children. Ain't you ever read your Bible?"

As the sheriff was leading the thief through the lobby where a crowd had gathered, Uncle Hank rushed in the front door. His face and hands were black and his trousers were stiff with dirt.

"Dan, Judd?" he called. "You boys all right? Word's all up and down Main Street that someone tried to hurt you."

Judd ran into his uncle's arms. "The knife was *this* big. I would've cut him if he'd hurt Danny. What's that,

Uncle?" He pointed to Hank's ears, which had white liquid dripping out and down into his beard.

"Oh, that's just candle wax, fella, don't worry. It's so noisy in the mill we have to plug our ears. Then it's hot, too, that's why it melts. Say, I am so glad you fellas aren't hurt."

"Can I go with you, Uncle Hank?" Judd had recovered from his encounter with the thief; in fact, he suddenly felt very brave. "I want to see what you do, Uncle, and I want to go down into a mine."

Madame came over with a peppermint stick for Judd. Her face was flushed from the excitement and despite the dark hair on her upper lip she looked pretty.

"I am proud of my sweet boy, so brave you are, darling. 'Allo, sir." She dipped her head slightly in greeting. "Your nephews are fine young men, and I am so very fond of then."

"Thank you, Madame." Uncle Hank looked down at Judd with a wink, then waved Danny over. "Fellas, how about this Tuesday? It's my day off and I could give you both a tour then."

It was hard for Danny to meet his eyes. If only his uncle weren't so nice to them it would be easier not to like him. Danny felt more confused than ever. He'd noticed that every time Uncle Hank was around, Judd seemed to be the happiest kid alive. The miner standing before them in stinking clothes obviously cared deeply for both of them.

Danny was beginning to understand that protecting his brother was one thing, helping him feel secure was another. He tried to hide the growing affection he had for his uncle, so he gave him the smallest of smiles.

"Tuesday's good, Uncle Hank."

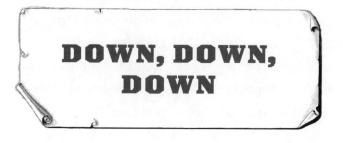

DOWN, DOWN, DOWN

UNCLE HANK HAD WORKED at Standard Mill for a year and, like many of the other men, he was gradually growing deaf from the noise and from the beeswax melting into his eardrums. The year before, he helped run the elevators that took men down into Standard Mine.

"Howdy, Frank, Bill," he called to his friends at the mine's entrance. "These here're my nephews; gonna show them some sparkle."

A shaft house covered the mine so that from the outside it appeared to be a store or school. Inside was a room where rows of coats and trousers hung against the walls. Hank peeled off his shirt and hooked it on a nail. His bare chest and arms were muscled like the beautiful marble statues Danny had seen in art museums.

Noticing Danny's stare, Uncle Hank said, "This is the changing room, boys, most of the bigger mines have them. For one thing it's hot as Hades the deeper you go, and the other thing is sometimes fellas try to smuggle gold in their pockets. We won't be down there long, but you still need to take off your shirts."

The brothers were white as fish bellies, their necks and hands dark brown, as were the other miners who were undressing. In another room two blacksmiths worked over a furnace. One was forging iron rails to be used as tracks down in the tunnels; another was repairing a rusted ore cart.

In the center of the shaft house there was an elevator for transporting miners up and down with their tools and sacks of ore. Another shaft was for the pump where hoses made from rubber canvas hung down like long strands of spaghetti, down hundreds of feet to the bottom, where water seeped out from the dark earth. Hank explained that without the pump the mine would flood and men could drown in minutes.

"Now whatever you do," he said, "keep your hands and feet inside the cage — your head, too. There ain't an inch to spare on either side so anything sticking out while we're going down will hit the wall. Saw a foreman once who bent over to tie his boot, but his shoulder caught a timber. He was mincemeat by the time the fellas on the bottom found him, dead, that is. Here we go, step in."

Short planks of wood lined the bottom of the narrow cage. Hank held his nephews close to him. Two sides were completely open and in place of a roof there was an iron wheel holding the cable. This cable led to a hoist that was operated by a noisy, puffing steam engine. A ten-year-old boy was feeding firewood into the engine's boiler.

Danny reached out to touch the hard dirt of the shaft, but quickly pulled in his arms when a whistle sounded.

"Ready!" Hank called to the hoistman.

A bell clanged four times. Danny felt a sudden rush of warm air as the cage slid down its cables, the sides of the shaft rushing upward at such a speed he felt his heart race. He caught his cap just as the wind lifted it off his head.

It was pitch-black for a few seconds, then there was a flash of light as they passed a crosscut on the one hundred-foot level. For an instant Danny saw miners working by candlelight, picks in hand, then it was black again. They slid downward in darkness, at every level glimpsing light from the tunnels.

A clang of a bell echoed from overhead, a faraway signal telling the operator to pull the brake. With a thump and a loud clatter, the cage stopped.

Hank led them out into a passageway dimly lit by a lantern hanging from the wall. Mud sucked at their shoes as they walked between the rail tracks, and warm water dripped onto Danny's bare back. He ran his hands along the damp walls and was surprised at the heat, like touching a stove after supper when the fire's burned low.

Every few feet they passed thick, squared timbers that formed upside down U's, designed to keep the tunnel from caving in. They followed Uncle Hank through a maze as he crouched under the beams, turned left, went straight ahead twenty feet, then around a corner up a muddy incline, ducking under a ledge. When they stepped into a room as tall and wide as a church, Danny gasped at the sight.

Candlelight reflected off specks of ore embedded in the rock. A ribbon of gold quartz three feet wide ran the length of the room along one wall, up the ceiling, where it disappeared around a dark corner. Men with picks were hacking at the walls with loud, rhythmic clinks that sounded like clocks ticking.

The men were naked except for skivvies cut off above the knees, and some wore skullcaps made from hats with the brims torn off. Boots kept their feet from being cut on the sharp floor. Sweat glistened on their skin.

Hank shouted above the noise, motioning his

nephews to follow him. Carved into one of the walls was a corral with bales of hay and a feeding trough. Nearby was a mule wearing a harness, pulling a cart of ore along the narrow iron tracks. It was headed for the maze that led to the elevators.

"That's Bessie," Hank yelled. "Came down here when she was a yearling, but she's grow'd so big, we can't haul 'er back up. She'll just live out her days here, good ol' Bessie."

A loud pop drew their attention to a wall where men had drilled a hole, filled it with black powder, then lit a fuse. The blast had lengthened the tunnel by twelve inches.

"It'll take those fellas all day to go ten feet," Hank continued to shout. Danny wanted to offer advice on how to make a bigger hole faster, but remembered they were more than five hundred feet inside the earth. An explosion like Smokey Joe's would be spectacular, but it would bury them alive.

Uncle Hank scraped his fingers against a wall, pulling out chunks of crumbly rock. By yelling above the noise he explained this mixture of clay and quartz would be sacked and hoisted up the elevator, carted to the mill, then crushed until the gold was squeezed out.

As the boys followed their uncle back toward the tunnel they noticed the miners' lunch pails off to the side.

Large gray rats were crawling over the pails, trying to open the lids with their claws and sharp teeth. Danny scooped up a handful of stones and took aim.

He felt sad for Bessie. The mule would never again see daylight and, worst of all, if the miners went home at night she would be down here alone with these terrible creatures.

TOO MUCH NOISE

RIDING UP THE ELEVATOR took longer than going down. The cables creaked and groaned while Uncle Hank explained things they would see next in the mill. He also told about accidents, terrible ones that happened many times each month.

In the changing room Hank handed the boys their shirts. "The other day," he said, "there was a poor old dog that jumped over Tioga shaft, but the dog slipped and fell. Down it went about one hundred feet, killing two men riding up. One time a fella dropped his hammer . . . well, my boys, you get the idea how dangerous things are."

As Hank buttoned his sleeves he said, "I don't want anything to happen to you, so don't ever, ever go down there without me, hear?"

From the shaft house they walked downhill in the warm August sunshine. Twenty feet overhead was a cable, stretched between towers, with ore buckets slowly moving down from the mine to the mill. One at a time, hinged doors on the bottom of each bucket clicked open to dump its contents.

Uncle Hank shaded his eyes with his hand as he studied the towers. "Boys," he said, "since you're from San-Fran-Sisco you've probably ridden on the cable cars. Well, their inventor, Mr. Andrew Hallidie, he came up here to Bodie and designed this tram for us. It saves us many hours of hard work. Here we are, I'll show you inside."

Standard Mill was such a huge building it looked like a wooden mansion pressed into the side of the hill. Hank led his nephews through the boiler room, where he shouted to explain that at least twenty cords of wood were burned every single day to make steam for powering the machines.

When they passed the flywheel, the noise was so great Hank just pointed. Danny had never seen such a huge turning wheel, solid iron, eighteen feet across. He tried to imagine the mule teams pulling such equipment up through the mountains.

The noise grew louder. Judd covered his ears as they climbed a long, narrow flight of stairs. The steps were worn smooth in the center, and along the edges there were piles of rat droppings. Tall windows, many of them broken from rocks and stray bullets, faced the barren hills. Wind whistled through the rafters where spiderwebs swayed overhead like tiny lace kites.

The stamp room was as large as a gymnasium. A row of posts — twenty of them — moved up and down, like men marching in place, iron upon iron, crushing ore that moments before had been dropped from the buckets. The noise was unbearable. Danny had a headache, and he worried about Judd who looked as if he were about to cry.

How could Uncle Hank work here day after day? Apparently the workers all plugged their ears with wax because each had white liquid dripping into his beard. Danny watched men with long-handled spoons shovel the crushed ore into pans of mercury where it would cook for hours with other chemicals, then drain into settling tanks. He knew that somehow the gold separated itself and would then be taken to the assayer for testing. An underground spring half a mile away supplied water that flushed the leftover rocks, called tailings, out of the mill. Bodie's younger children loved to swim in these tailings ponds, and in winter it was a popular place for ice-skating.

Something was troubling Danny, but because of his

headache it was hard to think. He remembered a day early this summer. In the law office he'd overheard a conversation between Mr. Reddy and the undertaker. It seems that several children had recently died from mercury poisoning and the two men worried it might be because of the ponds.

Now summer was nearly over. Danny wondered if anyone had told children not to swim there. Maybe he himself should have posted a warning, but truth was he hadn't remembered mercury was poison until just now.

He looked at the top step where Judd was sitting, but the boy was now sobbing, his small hands pressed against his ears, eyes squeezed shut. Danny tugged on Uncle Hank's shirt, then pointed to his little brother.

Hank rushed over to Judd and picked him up, holding him against his shoulder. Nodding to Danny, he hurried down the stairs, past the flywheel, through the boiler room, then outside. Taking Judd's hand, he led his nephews across the bluff to his cabin at the top of Green Street.

"I am so sorry," he said to Judd, kneeling to brush dirt from the boy's shirt. "That's just too much noise for any human being. Come in, let's have something to eat."

The door was open to let in the afternoon sunlight. Danny peered in and noticed the cabin was tidy and there was the delicious aroma of fresh-baked apple pie.

Instead of bunks there now was one bed in the corner with a drape for privacy. The burlap curtains had been replaced with soft, white calico, which gave the room a cheerful appearance. Blue enamel cookware hung from a rafter. On a shelf were rows of small bottles containing herbs and spices.

Lu-Chen was by the stove. She gave Judd a tender look and when she held out her arms he ran to her, crying louder than before. As she stroked his forehead, Danny saw the ring on her left finger.

They were married!

He ran out the door. As he hurried away he could hear his uncle calling after him.

"Son, come back, please," cried Hank.

Danny hid at Tuolumne Sawmill, between the barn and stacks of lumber. No one could hear him weeping. He hated Hank for going through with the wedding and he hated Lu-Chen for being nice to them.

But what confused Danny most of all was something he just now realized: It felt good, so good, to once again be called "son" by someone who cared about him.

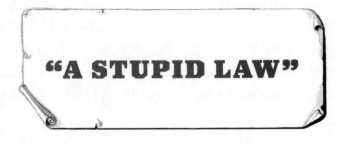

"A STUPID LAW"

DANNY WOKE UP the next morning with Judd curled under the blanket next to him. Uncle Hank must have brought him down to the hotel sometime in the night. For an instant he wanted also to hate his little brother for being a traitor. How could he like Lu-Chen so much . . . didn't he know she was Chinese?

He crept out from under the billiard table and hurriedly ate Madame's breakfast. She patted his cheek and smiled, but did not ask why he seemed upset.

At City Market he washed down the butcher's counter then swept the sidewalk for there was always a mess from the swallows that nested in the eaves overhead. Finally he delivered a sack of fresh bread to Clara's Boardinghouse. He wanted to tell Stella about the marriage, but she was rushing back and forth from the kitchen to the parlor where customers waited for breakfast.

When she passed him carrying a plate of fried ham she whispered, "Come back at ten, Danny, and we can go for a walk."

"All right," he said. Meanwhile, there was someone else he could talk to.

Pat Reddy leaned back in his chair, his arm behind his head, his empty sleeve at his side. He looked at Danny with kindness.

"I know how upset ye are, laddie, but let me show you something."

He walked to the bookcase, stepped up the ladder, and pulled down a thick, yellow volume that he opened on his desk. Humming a tune, he flipped through the index.

"Aha! Here 'tis, m'boy. Read it to me, why don't you." The lawyer tapped the page.

Danny studied the words, then looked down at the bare floor. "I can't read those big sentences, sir," he said.

Mr. Reddy nodded. "All right, then, just listen. This is the Fourteenth Amendment to the Constitution: 'All persons born in the United States are citizens of the United States and of the State wherein they reside. No State shall . . . deprive any person of life, liberty, or property, without due process of law. . . .'

"Danny, this law has been in place since 1868 —

that's eleven years ago. You might also be surprised to learn that the Fifteenth Amendment says any American citizen can vote no matter their race or color, even if they'd been a slave. If Lu-Chen were a man, she could vote. Fancy that."

Danny was quiet. He looked out the window to the busy street below. Finally he said, "Since Lu-Chen was born in San Francisco, she really is an American? She told me her parents are from China, by the Pearl River Delta." To himself he thought, This is a stupid law.

"Yes, laddie, that's what our Constitution says."

"But isn't there a law against them getting married?"

Mr. Reddy opened another book on his desk and thumbed through the pages. "What you're thinking of, lad, is called miscegenation, marriage between races. In fact, most of the Southern states have laws forbidding this between Negroes and whites. Now, Lu-chen could have married one of the Paiutes who live here and folks wouldn't get upset, but because she married a white man, that's another story. But let me ask you something. Sit down."

Danny lowered himself into the chair by the window. Morning sunlight washed the room in heat, made bearable by the ceiling fans. "Yes, sir?"

"Clearly your uncle and Lu-Chen are devoted to each other. What would you do if California had such a law?"

Danny looked at the palms of his hands, then shrugged. His voice was dry. "I don't know," he whispered.

"You're a bright lad, Danny, but there are two things I want you to carefully consider. Number one: There's no excuse for not being able to read better; get yourself back in school, your brother, too. When you are well read, you'll never be lonely, but more important, you'll never be ignorant.

"Second thing: The way you're treating Lu-Chen and your uncle is called prejudice. Prejudice is a great time-saver, laddie. It allows you to form an opinion without getting all the facts."

Mr. Reddy sat on the edge of his desk and smiled at Danny. "Now run along, m'boy, and stop worrying about such rubbish. Let your mind dwell on things that are true and noble."

Summer came to a quick end when snow fell during the first week of September. Wind chilled the hillsides and brought a call for more firewood to the hotels and rooming houses. At night Captain Billy spread extra blankets over his sleeping boys, and he kept the stove blazing.

During a stormy afternoon Danny sat in front of the fire. He was thinking about what Mr. Reddy had told

him. Maybe it was true about going back to school —
certainly his parents would have been pleased. Suddenly Danny realized that both he and Judd had forgotten their birthdays in July; he was now thirteen and
his brother seven. How he missed his dear mother! She
would always tuck a present under his pillow with a
note written to him in her beautiful handwriting.

A shout interrupted his thoughts. Captain Billy
rushed into the lobby, waving his arms. Fresh snow covered his shoulders and hair.

"Madame is missing," he cried. "Two days now. I
checked at the Magnolia, but they thought she was
here . . . mercy, where can she be?"

Danny felt sick inside. Lately he'd been so busy with
his own troubles, he'd not noticed that Madame Mustache hadn't greeted him at breakfast. It hadn't occurred
to him to ask Captain Billy about her.

His face burned with shame. How selfish he'd been.

"I'll help you look." He pulled his wool sweater down
over his head and put on his cap. Setting aside his anger
toward Smokey Joe he called him over. "Come on, Joe,"
he said, "let's get Captain Billy's wagon."

THE LAST STRAW

CAPTAIN BILLY SNAPPED the reins as he pulled his small wagon out of the livery stable. Snow was falling so fast it appeared the horse was wearing a thick, white robe.

"Ee-up!" he shouted. Danny and Smokey Joe rode up on the seat with him, a blanket over their shoulders to keep off the snow. They headed west out of town, toward Bridgeport for that's where folks said Madame might have gone.

As soon as word spread about her being missing, Big Bertha had rushed through the blizzard into the hotel and shook out her snowy cape. In tears, she told a story that so upset Captain Billy he sunk to the floor, his hands trembling in his lap.

It seems the previous day Madame had been dealing a high-stakes poker game. Things apparently were going poorly for one of the gamblers, so when he lost he stood up and made a cruel speech, loud enough for everyone in the saloon to hear.

"I don't mind losing," the man had said, *"but I'll be blasted if I lose to a woman that's ugly as a dog."*

"Madame herself stood up," related Big Bertha. "She drew a pistol out of her sleeve and aimed at the man, but instead of shooting him she threw it into the pile of money that was on the table. She grabbed her cloak from the hallway, then hurried outside.

"I thought she was coming here, Billy, so I didn't follow her. It was only this morning that my cook said he'd seen her out on the road, walking alone, but mercy, Bridgeport's fifteen miles away." At this Big Bertha wept into her hands.

Captain Billy leaned forward to see better through the blowing snow. Tall weeds on the right side were the only clue they were still on the road.

Suddenly Danny pointed. "Stop!" he cried. He and Smokey Joe jumped down into a drift and ran with great steps toward what looked like a pile of coal. They brushed away the snow.

The lifeless eyes of Madame Mustache stared up at them, her face framed by the black hood of her cape. The boys tried to lift her, but she was heavy with ice.

"Oh . . . ohh," wailed Captain Billy. He put his arm

under her shoulders and pulled her to him. He rocked with sorrow. "My beauty," he said, "now no one can hurt you anymore."

The lobby of the Occidental Hotel was crowded with mourners. Uncle Hank came in with another armload of logs for the fire. Lu-Chen was there, too, pressing a cup of hot coffee into Captain Billy's cold hands.

Danny was heartbroken. *What had happened?* everyone was asking one another. *Why did Madame run away during a blizzard? She knew better. . . .*

After Captain Billy had stopped shivering, he began to talk in a low voice.

"Guess it was the straw that broke the camel's back," he said. "Every day someone would make fun of her, every single day. But she just keep on going, smiling her heartache away. . . ." Tears filled his eyes.

"Once long ago, you see, she had a husband and a baby, but they died of measles. You chillen, you all helped fill Madame's lonely heart. . . ." His voice breaking, Captain Billy covered his face with his handkerchief.

Big Bertha put her arms around him. To comfort him and the children she had brought over sandwiches from her kitchen and a kettle of soup to set on Billy's stove. Someone else carried in a tall jar of pickled eggs; cheese and salami came from City Market. While a storm raged outside, friends gathered around the fire to remember Madame Mustache, the popular croupier who had sailed to America from France as a young girl and made her living in mining camps throughout the West.

Danny watched Lu-Chen moving among the crowd with a tall coffeepot. Her long, black hair swung over her shoulder as she bent down to fill someone's cup. The way she glanced over at him with a smile made him feel good. He buttoned up his coat, put on his cap, then stepped out into the cold air. Hunching his shoulders against the wind, he walked along the snowy sidewalk through town.

He still couldn't believe Madame was dead. She hadn't meant to freeze to death, he was sure of it, but somehow she must have been so upset she hadn't realized she was putting herself in such danger.

He was deep in thought when a snowball burst against his arm.

"Where you going?" called Smokey Joe.

Danny looked up the hill to the schoolhouse. He wanted to try harder to get along with Smokey Joe. "I'm visiting Miss Polly, wanna come?"

"Not me. Hey, what's this about your uncle making family with a Chinese —"

Danny didn't let him finish. Changing his mind

about being friends, he grabbed the front of Smokey Joe's shirt, twisted it, and pulled him so close their noses touched.

"You shut your mouth," he said. With both hands Danny picked him up and threw him into a snowbank. Standing over the startled boy, he said, "My aunt is an American and if you ever talk bad about her again, or my uncle, I'll pound you."

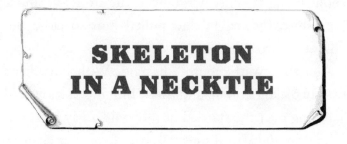

SKELETON
IN A NECKTIE

THE SECOND FLOOR of the schoolhouse had rows of desks facing a potbellied stove, and a wood box was in the center aisle. Wallboards covered with black oilcloth had the day's lessons written in chalk. A portrait of President Rutherford B. Hayes hung next to one of George Washington, and between them was an American flag with thirty-eight stars.

Danny gazed out the south-facing windows where snow-covered hills looked perfect for sledding. He opened his book with a sigh. He would try harder to read better. He would do it for Mr. Reddy and for his parents, and to be an example for Judd. Madame also would have been pleased to see him in school.

At noon the children clamored downstairs to get their coats and lunch pails. Some lined up to use the outhouse; others immediately formed teams to do battle with snowballs.

Danny watched with curiosity as a boy ran uphill toward school. When he saw it was Smokey Joe he turned away. Sometimes it was easy to be nice to him; sometimes it wasn't.

Out of breath, Smokey Joe caught up to him. "Danny," he said, "guess what I found. A skeleton, a real one, it's an old prospector, I think. Wanna see it?"

"Where?"

Smokey Joe pointed toward Mono Lake. "But we have to hurry. Sheriff Kirgan saw it, too, and he's getting some men together."

Danny made a quick decision. It had been a long time since he'd done anything fun. They'd all missed Hidalgo Day because it was so soon after Madame's funeral, and he'd been attending school for a whole month. What harm was there in playing hooky for an afternoon?

He found Judd making a snowman with his new friends. "Stay here," Danny said to him. "I'll see you at supper."

One mile southwest of town they came to a ravine that was protected from the cold wind. Danny couldn't believe his eyes.

Stretched out on an old horse blanket was a man's skeleton. The skull had perfect teeth. A rotting silk necktie lay over the ribcage, and around the waist was a leather scabbard with a knife.

Smokey Joe examined the knife by pushing it with a rock. One side of the hilt was engraved with a woman's head; a lion was on the other side. A well-preserved shoe was attached to the right foot.

Danny stared in fascination. Before he could think of what to say, they saw a group of men approaching on the ridge. Soon Judge McClinton was there with editors from three of the town's newspapers and several other men. They all stared down at the skeleton. An older man with a thick gray beard knelt in the snow, carefully studying the knife.

"Well, I'll be," he said. "I do believe this is Old Man Bodey hisself. This was his knife — see the way this scabbard is fastened with bullet rivets? I was there when he made it." Looking around at the landmarks he nodded.

"This must be him, poor fellow, right where Black Taylor and Johnson King said they buried him. Twenty years ago, can you believe it?"

The skeleton was put into a coffin, then lifted into the undertaker's hearse, a long black carriage with windows on its sides. Four black horses led a procession through town to the cemetery where a hole had been dynamited into the frozen earth.

William S. Bodey's funeral was held on the first Sunday in November, a cold afternoon with clouds low in the sky. Nearly the entire town closed up shop to attend. Eloquent speeches were made on behalf of the first prospector to stake a claim in these hills.

The town was even named for him. When Danny heard that many years ago a sign painter had misspelled Bodey's name he wondered if it had been because the painter didn't know how to read.

Another thing he wondered about was why did thousands of people show up at Mr. Bodey's funeral — people who'd never met him — simply because he had discovered gold? Yet a few weeks ago Madame, who had been kind and generous and loved by many, had been quietly buried next to Buster, an orphan of little notice. There had been no speeches or cannons fired, no parade through town.

On the day of Mr. Bodey's funeral Danny asked Uncle Hank his opinion on the matter. They stood in front of the Bodie Opera House, watching a column of gray-headed miners march by.

"Son," he said after thinking a moment, "Madame had a heart of gold, which is far more valuable than gold itself. But judging by these two funerals I'd wager that most folks in town don't know the difference."

EPIDEMIC

As SNOW FELL STEADILY, fewer and fewer travelers came to Bodie. Mountain passes were buried. Only the most foolhardy mule skinner tried to plow his way through.

The first time Danny noticed something was wrong was when a dozen new coffins were delivered from the sawmill to the undertaker. They were stacked out front on the sidewalk, many only about four feet long, the size of a child. He reported this to Captain Billy.

"It's pneumonia, Danny," he said. "So many have died, they're calling it an epidemic. Just take care that you and your brother stay warm."

Danny stared in the undertaker's window with morbid curiosity. He was terrified of an epidemic, for that was what had killed his mother and father and most of their neighbors. How could pneumonia find its way up here, so far from anywhere?

Standing on a crate he boosted himself up to get a better look. One of the coffins was opened, revealing a redheaded boy he'd seen in school. His eyes were closed, his face like wax. Danny hadn't realized the boy was even sick, for he'd seen him just the other day. Three other coffins were open, but they held the bodies of men he didn't recognize.

The next day Danny again climbed onto the windowsill. There were bodies of two more children and two women, all sudden victims of pneumonia, according to a handwritten note on the door. Looking north of town he could see that the cemetery was pocked with freshly dug graves.

Day by day Danny's classroom had more empty desks. Miss Polly began each morning with prayer for those who were home ill, then prayer for the families whose child had died. *Tommy, Sid, Ned, Alice* . . . Hearing their names filled Danny with dread. Who would be next?

November 17 was a dark, windy day. Snow blew under the door and through cracks in the walls. Miss Polly erased the blackboard with a rag then turned to face her students.

"Class," she said, "you must stay warm, especially keep your feet dry. Sheriff Kirgan told me this morning that twenty-nine people died in October, and so far this month twenty have passed away.

Because of the cold the children ate lunch downstairs in the music room. There was much noise from the piano as five girls arranged themselves on the bench to play a song together. A rubber ball was being bounced against a wall by several loud boys; some quieter children played dominoes and checkers.

When Danny saw Judd staring out the window, his lunch pail in his lap unopened, he sat down next to him.

"Judd?"

He turned toward Danny, but his eyes were glazed, his face flushed. In alarm Danny felt his brother's cheeks.

"Judd, you're burning up. Miss Polly!"

The room fell silent. Miss Polly helped button Judd into his coat and wrap a muffler around his neck. She put warm wool socks on his feet that had been drying by the stove, then tied his shoes. The children watched quietly as Danny lifted him onto his hip and hurried outside into the blizzard.

Captain Billy dipped a cloth into a bowl of melting snow, wrung it out, then lay it over Judd's hot forehead.

Danny stood anxiously over the couch where his brother tossed feverishly. How he wished Madame Mustache would come through the door. She would be so worried, so caring. Danny choked back tears. He missed her and he was afraid.

Please don't die, Judd.

As the day wore on Judd's breathing grew heavy, as if he were panting. When he briefly opened his eyes, he saw Danny kneeling at his side.

"Dan," he whispered, "my chest hurts."

"Don't worry, you're going to be all right."

He tucked another blanket around Judd for he was shivering, then went to the stove where Captain Billy was loading in more wood.

"I don't know what to do," said Danny.

Captain Billy brushed soot from his palms, then reached for his coat hanging on the wall. "You jess sit tight. I'll go find the doc."

An hour passed. Wind shrieked against the building. Danny was pacing when Captain Billy finally returned. Ice was crusted on his chin and in his hair.

"I'm sorry, Danny. The good doctor is somewhere in town, but so many's sick, I couldn't find him."

Danny looked at his brother and swallowed hard. "But if we don't get help . . ."

Captain Billy nodded. A tear rolled down his cheek.

I am not going to lose my brother, Danny thought angrily. He buttoned up his coat, tied his cap under his chin, and found Smokey Joe.

"Joe, I need you. Hurry."

HOME

WITH CAPTAIN BILLY'S HELP the boys wrapped Judd in three blankets, one forming a hood over his head, another for a sling.

Danny knew the only hope was to take him to Lu-Chen. He'd heard how Chinese have healing ways and he'd seen her bottles of herbs. And he didn't care if Smokey Joe liked it or not.

While Captain Billy stayed behind to continue searching for the doctor, the boys carried Judd out into the storm. With snow blowing in their faces, they huddled together, Judd between them, and jogged up Green Street. Not a word passed between them, and when they arrived at Uncle Hank's cabin they were out of breath.

With his mittened hand Danny pounded on the window. Light flooded out onto the snowy street when Hank opened the door. With one look he seemed to understand and he quickly helped the boys inside.

"He's sick, Uncle, real sick."

"You did good bringing him here, son." Uncle Hank peeled away the blankets and took Judd's face in his hands. He leaned down to listen to the boy's chest. A rattling sound came with every breath.

Lu-Chen took her kettle from the stove and poured steaming water into a bowl. From a shelf she took down a basket and scooped out a handful of leaves, which she crushed between her fingers. These she sprinkled into the water along with a pinch of herbs from two little bottles.

Instantly the minty aroma of eucalyptus filled the small room. She carried the bowl to a stool by the bed where Judd lay.

"Hold him up," she said to Smokey Joe, motioning him to push Judd into a sitting position, then support him from behind. She showed Hank how to hold a towel over Judd's head so he could breathe in the healing steam.

"Danny, sit by me so your brother can see you. Keep talking to him. I'll keep the water hot. There's a good boy, Judd," she said, stroking his damp hair from his forehead. "You'll be fine, my little friend. Stay with us."

Danny woke suddenly. He was surprised to find himself and Smokey Joe lying on a straw mat in front of the stove, the warm skin of a mountain lion spread over them. A lantern glowed from the shelf in the corner. Uncle Hank sat in bed with Judd cradled in his arms, Judd breathing heavily but sound asleep. Lu-Chen was pressing dough into a pan for biscuits.

"His fever's gone," she said when she noticed Danny was awake. "But he'll need to stay with us until he's well. Danny, we almost lost him."

We.

Danny was too exhausted to think, but something settled within him when Lu-Chen said *we almost lost him.* With a new contentment he realized he was no longer alone in trying to care for his brother.

He watched Lu-Chen pour brown sugar into a bowl of porridge. She handed it to Danny with a spoon. Her hair was combed into one long braid this morning, tied at the end with red string, and though she hadn't slept all night she was cheerful.

Danny was tired of struggling, especially against her and against Uncle Hank. So what if she's Chinese? he thought. She's Lu-Chen.

She loves Uncle Hank, she loves Judd, and — Danny took a deep breath — I think she loves me.

ANOTHER CHRISTMAS

THE OCCIDENTAL HOTEL was cheerful with decorations: Strings of cranberries and popped corn hung in the windows, and in the center of the lobby there was a fresh-cut pine tree standing in a bucket. An aroma of gingerbread came from the kitchen where Danny was helping Captain Billy roll out dough for cookies.

"Well, my friend, I sure am glad to see you again," the old black man said. "Yessir, I am."

Smokey Joe came in from the back porch, carrying a pail of snow to melt on the stove. He set it carefully over the flame. "So, you're staying with your uncle now?" he said.

"Yes, Joe, we are."

Several moments passed with only the noise of billiards coming from the next room. The boys watched Captain Billy crack five eggs, one by one, into a bowl of flour then beat the mixture with a long wooden spoon. Finally Smokey Joe cleared his throat. "Well, guess I'll see you later, maybe tonight."

"All right," said Danny. He was relieved that for once they hadn't exchanged hard words.

Danny was still surprised he had moved in with Uncle Hank and Lu-Chen, and even more surprised he felt happy there.

Everything had happened so fast.

The night Judd was ill, Uncle Hank insisted his nephews come live with him immediately. So when it stopped snowing Danny returned to the hotel, packed a small bag with his and Judd's few belongings, then hiked back up the hill. While his brother slept, Danny helped Lu-Chen rearrange the cabin. Now they had their own warm bed by the stove with two pegs in the wall to hang their clothes.

A few weeks later, on Christmas morning, Danny received another surprise. Lu-Chen was pouring hot cranberry juice into their cups when Hank came in through the front door, his arms loaded with firewood.

"Man, it's cold out there, twenty-three degrees below zero," he said. After stacking the wood against the back wall he took off his gloves then bent down to feel Judd's forehead. "No fever, but his cough worries me. Danny, he needs warmer weather."

Hank pulled a letter from his pocket. "This here's from my brother, your uncle Adam. Well, he just moved to Mammoth City with his wife and little girls, and opened a mercantile. He wants me to be his partner. What I'm getting at is this, son: Mammoth is in the lower mountains — maybe forty miles from here as the crow flies — but not near as cold as Bodie."

Melting ice dripped from Hank's beard. He put his hand on Danny's shoulder. "Lu-Chen and I want you boys to come with us. Mammoth has hot springs for taking the cure, and there's a school so you can finish your learning. We'll be good to you, I promise. For me and your uncle Adam, having you will be like having part of our sister back."

The day before they were to leave, Danny visited Stella at the boardinghouse. She put her hands on her hips and looked at him with her blue eyes. "I'm going to come visit you," she said, "and we'll swim in the hot springs."

"No you're not," he answered. "It ain't proper for a girl to look up a boy."

"Well, smarty, I guess you don't know that 1880 is a leap year, so there. I can do whatever I like."

"All right, Stella." He held out his hand to shake hers, but she turned away and hurried into the kitchen.

Danny walked out, then cupped his hands against the front window for one last look inside. If only Stella could come, too.

The sidewalks were icy. Though it was the middle of winter every store, saloon, and cafe was busy with people coming and going: miners, gamblers, ladies in cloaks and bonnets. Main Street was crowded with sleighs drawn by horses, clouds of frost puffing with every breath as they trotted through the snow. Along the rooftops smoke curled up from chimneys and stovepipes.

Down the side streets children were running with snowballs or dragging one another on sleds. Danny smiled at their fun. When Judd's feeling better, I'll help him build a snowman.

Mr. Reddy's office was closed. A note on the door said he was in Superior Court at Bridgeport until January 5. Danny wished he had thanked the lawyer for his kindness, but decided he could do so in a letter when he got to Mammoth.

At the Occidental, Captain Billy was in the kitchen. While he was taking bread out of the oven, Danny snuck into the parlor where the man's coat was hanging on the back of a chair. Quickly he hid five silver dollars and ten five-dollar notes in one of the pockets. It was the only way he knew to repay him because Billy had refused to accept money all these months.

Danny stood by the pantry to say good-bye. "Thank you, Captain Billy," he said. "Thank you for everything."

The man gave Danny a paper sack filled with fresh baked brownies, then shook his hand. "You did real good, boy, taking care of your brother and yourself. Now I can stop worrying about you. Go on now, get."

"Yes, sir. But first I need to see Smokey Joe."

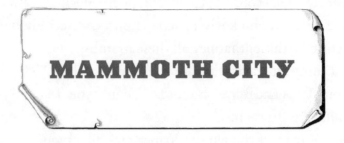

MAMMOTH CITY

Danny found Smokey Joe upstairs sweeping the long hallway. Sunlight pooled on the floor between them, slanting in from a window overhead. The boys looked at each other for a moment then Danny nervously took off his cap and fingered its brim.

"Joe," he said, "we'd like you to come with us. Uncle Hank said you're welcome, that there's plenty of space. I think me and you, we'd get along just fine if we try hard."

Smokey Joe leaned against his broom. "Your uncle said that, really?"

"Yes. He also said he won't leave you an orphan, that there's always a home for you it you want. Well, I gotta go, we're leaving tomorrow morning early. Joe, the ticket costs eight dollars and I will gladly pay for yours myself."

The sleigh pulled south through town. Sun glistened off the snow. The air was still and cold. Danny rode on

142

the seat with Uncle Hank, looking back every few minutes to see if Smokey Joe was running after them. Or to see something that might make Danny change his mind about leaving Bodie. But there were only the icy white hills and sky so blue and chilled it took his breath away. Judd was in the sleigh, warm next to Lu-Chen, nestled out of the wind among the various trunks and satchels that held their belongings.

The day before, Uncle Hank had tried to prepare Danny for their new life. "Many folks hate Lu-Chen because she's Chinese," he said. "And they hate me because I dared to marry her. We just have to live with it, that's all."

Danny watched the scenery glide by, the ring of their sleighbells echoing across the frozen landscape. Far to the west lay the jagged peaks of the Sierra Nevada, white with cliffs of rock showing through. Ahead was Mono Lake where they had camped last spring, gray and flat as a coin, and nearby were its extinct craters. In the snow along the trail there were tracks from a rabbit that disappeared under a sagebrush, the only sign they were not alone on this vast snowy desert.

They stayed the night with a rancher who wouldn't look at Lu-Chen or offer her food, but who did allow her to sleep inside on the kitchen floor. This made

Danny mad. He didn't know what to do about it except to share his own supper with Lu-Chen and try not to punch the rancher in the jaw. Was this what Uncle Hank meant by living with prejudice?

The next morning they continued their journey. The driver of a sleigh approaching from the other direction yelled, "Hello!" as he passed in a spray of snow. His horses wore the proud red harnesses of Mammoth Lakes Lightning Mail.

As they followed the road, Uncle Hank pointed to a thin trail cutting up into the foothills. "Tioga Pass, Danny, goes high into the Sierra then down into Yosemite Valley. I'll take you and Judd there this summer, but right now the snow's forty feet deep at the summit. Matter of fact, all these mountain passes are buried."

Soon they were upon forests of lodgepole pine, towering spruce, and aspen. A porcupine waddled across the trail then climbed a tree. This bothered two blue jays who flew from the branches with noisy squawks. Finally around a bend the woods opened up to a valley. Compared to Bodie, Mammoth looked like a village, not a city. But Danny didn't care.

He hoped Mother would be pleased that he and Judd were safe, that two of her own brothers would be looking after them. And Danny knew Father would be proud of the way he'd found a new family.

Exhaustion settled over Danny. For several days he slept long hours, waking only to check on Judd and accept the broth Lu-Chen spooned into him. When he looked out the window by his bed he saw a winter wonderland and marveled at the stillness. No pounding stamp mill, no saloon music all night long, no gunshots.

He slept and dreamed.

Soon enough the brothers ventured out on snowshoes. Their new home was a cabin built of logs felled from the forest. Large gray stones formed the fireplace and chimney, stones taken from a nearby river. Behind the cabin was a creek, frozen now, which stretched through the woods like a silvery snake. Danny had never seen such a beautiful place.

After breakfast one morning, Lu-Chen gave Danny the paper and envelopes he'd asked for. He had three letters to send.

Dipping his pen into a pot of ink he first wrote to Mr. Reddy. In his very best penmanship he thanked the kind lawyer then told him about school and about his new family.

Next, he wrote Smokey Joe. *You have a home with us,* he told him. *Judd and I sleep in the loft over the kitchen. It's warm and there's plenty of room for you. Don't mind Lu-Chen, she's good to us and she will be good to you. Please come.*

His third letter was the longest.

Two nuns dressed in dark, brown wool sat together in a courtyard where a fountain bubbled down into a pond. One of them carefully unfolded a letter that had arrived that morning and read it aloud to the two-year-old girl playing at their feet. This is what it said:

Mammoth City, California
January 22, 1880

Dear Susanna,

I know you are too small to read this yourself, but maybe Sister Mary Catherine will read it to you. In spring, Uncle Hank and I will come for you. We will wait for the snow to melt on Sonora Pass, then we will come by stage. It will take us forty hours, but we will come.

You will like our new home, Susanna. We have three girl cousins waiting to meet you and a new mother. Judd misses you. So do I.

Your brother,
Daniel.

AUTHOR'S NOTE

ORPHAN RUNAWAYS is fiction based on many true characters and real events.

Madame Mustache's real name was Eleanor Dumont and she did die two miles from Bodie, on the road to Bridgeport; it is thought she committed suicide because "an empty poison vial" was found at her side. An obituary dated September 13, 1879, in the *Esmeralda Herald* in Aurora, Nevada, gave a colorful description of her gambling life: She came to Nevada City from France in 1854, arriving "on a stagecoach, a pretty, fresh-faced, dark-eyed woman, apparently about twenty years of age. Her stylish appearance created much commotion among the rough inhabitants of the town. The novelty of a pretty woman dealing a game attracted many players to her table. . . . Of late years, what was in her girlhood only an infantile fuzz on the upper lip had developed into the growth of unusual proportions for a woman; hence the nickname, 'Madame Mustache.'"

"Captain" Billy O'Hara, a black man descended from slaves, was actually called "Uncle Billy," the Foster Father of Bodie. He was greatly respected because of his generosity and the way he cared for needy children. Before living in Aurora then Bodie, he was a personal steward to William C. Ralston, President of the Bank of California.

Patrick Reddy, the son of Irish immigrants, indeed lost his arm in a shootout, but historical records disagree which arm and in which town. Because I could not find a full-length photo of him, or a first-person description, I left that detail up to the reader's imagination. Mr. Reddy often donated his legal services to the poor and charged the rich double; he was well-known for treating destitute miners to luxurious dinners. He was a California state senator from 1883–1887.

In 1882 President Chester A. Arthur signed the Chinese Exclusion Act, which stated, *Hereafter no state court or court of The United States shall admit Chinese to citizenship.* The Act also suspended Chinese immigration. It was finally appealed in 1943.

An extra session of California's 33rd Legislature, held from January 29 through February 10, 1900, passed amendments to the statutes and codes, part of which reads: *All marriages of white persons with negroes, mongolians, or mulattoes are illegal and void.* Nearly fifty years later, antimiscegenation laws were found to be unconstitutional by the California Supreme Court in *Perez* v. *Sharp.*

Sheriff John F. Kirgan was a well-liked constable who kept a clean jail and served such good food the inmates called it "Hotel de Kirgan." He was killed in 1881 when his sulky overturned on Main Street.

The skeleton of Waterman S. Body (also known as William S. Bodey or Wakeman S. Bodey) was found outside of town in a shallow grave, some twenty years after two friends buried him when he died in a blizzard in Cottonwood Canyon. Some confusion exists as to the true spelling of his name (Body or Bodey), and how or why the town named after him is now spelled Bodie. Some say it was a sign painter's error; others say that citizens wanted to make sure it wasn't mispronounced. His funeral on November 2, 1879, was a flamboyant affair.

The pneumonia epidemic of fall 1879 was eventually believed to have been caused by bacteria from contaminated water. Poisons that seeped into the wells came from outhouses, the soaps and lye of Chinese laundries, and mercury from the tailing ponds, but most people of the day were unaware of these dangers.

Ten years after the gold rush of 1849 mining along the western slope of the Sierra Nevada began to decline. Prospectors headed east to Colorado, Nevada, Utah, and sites in the eastern Sierra. Bodie's boom was in 1880 when the population swelled to nearly 10,000. A year later there were only 3,000 residents, and by 1887 there were just 1,500. Most mines were closed by then and many vacant buildings were hauled away to other camps.

Designated a California State Historic Park in 1962, Bodie is considered an authentic gold-mining ghost town. Visitors can walk the dusty streets and imagine the town as it was in its heyday, although only five percent of the original buildings still remain. The park is open year-round.

I'm indebted to Dave Marquart and Susan DesBaillets from the California State Park Service for personally escorting me through Bodie's deserted stores, hotel, morgue, schoolhouse, and Standard Stamp Mill. Thanks also to research assistants and snack coordinators Adam Gardner, Chris Gardner, Karen Gardner, and Greg Rutty.